Introduction

I began this book in November of 2010. It was inspired by a small square on my left arm that changes from time to time and has never been explained by any doctors. They always say it must be some kind of mole, but always agree that the shape is interesting. I've always kidded people, and said that it was an alien implant. That's why I always intended this book to be a science fiction novel, and I still mostly do.

But in October of 2011, my wife and I were watching a show about UFOs on the television. I always like stuff about aliens and such because I do believe that in a universe the size of the one we live in, it just seems impossible that this little dot, called Earth, can be the only place with some sort of life on it. And I'm sure that I've seen some things in the sky that can't be explained. What stopped me cold though, was when they interviewed a retired Brazilian Air Force officer, who said he had been abducted by the aliens, and they had put an implant in his arm. The exact same shape, si⁊ ⁔or, and placement on his arm, as the m ⁔⁔
also said it changes, just like ⁔
had been different about his
then I could write it off as c⁔
was an exact match.

Now, I'm not ready to run out to the press and proclaim that I've been abducted by aliens, but it did put me in mind of Derek and Carl's first meeting in Chapter 2 of my little book here. And I was very surprised when I saw this mark on someone else in the world. The thing is, you just never know. So, with these thoughts in mind, and in the spirit of this book, if you happen to have a 3/16" X 3/16" square on the inside of your left forearm that goes from almost imperceptible, to dark brown and $1/16th - 1/8th$ of an inch high, email me at findtherest9474@gmail.com and let me know.

And if I don't hear anything from anyone else, then I'll know it was an incredible coincidence.

In any case, enjoy the book!

Chapter 1

Twenty after three. Good grief, thought Carl, what the hell am I doing looking at Orion's belt? But, it was a nice night. About 63 degrees, the smell of the autumn leaves wafting up on a gentle breeze. The full moon, just over Betelgeuse in Orion's right shoulder, gave the yard a silver/black glow. "I gotta go to bed", he said to himself. But before he could turn, his cell rang.

He looked at the number and softly chuckled. "What's up goofball?" "Hey, are you awake?", Derek asked.

"Yeah".

"Great, cause I got one for ya!".

"Just because I'm awake, doesn't mean I'm staying up, it *is* almost three-thirty in the morning. I gotta get some sleep." Carl said, all the while, knowing he'd be in the car in ten minutes. "Yeah, whatever, see you in a while", Derek said, and he hung up.

As he was getting ready to slip on a tee shirt, Carl looked at his arm and thought, maybe long sleeve today.

Chapter 2

Carl Haskins was a forty- five year old bachelor. He was a maintenance manager at a large auto parts factory, before he retired. Now, things were a little different.

For the last fourteen years he had been searching.

"So, whad'ya got?" Carl asked, five hours later, walking through the open door of the lab.

"German girl, 35, single, having crazy dreams. It sounds like she's remembering." Derek said, not taking his eyes off of the computer screen. "She was reported by her doctor, he's been with the group for about eight years."

After all of these years, Derek knew how to answer Carl's questions, usually before he asked them.

"She have a mark?"

Carl silently wondered how many there would be, in the end. 2,067, or 68, if this girl was for real, after all these years. People have been making claims for a hundred years, with only a small handful being the real deal. How many are there? What's going to happen to us? And when.

"Hey look!" Derek broke into his train of thought, "He got a picture of the chip. It looks right, and it's in the right place."

"Why did she go to the doctor, was it about the chip?" Carl asked, glaring at the image on the monitor.

"No, it was a routine exam. She's a new patient to him. He asked her about it, but she said she never paid much attention to it. She did say that it seems to change at times, but other than that, she's never worried about it. Her last doctor told her it was just some kind of benign mole." Derek read from the doctor's e-mail.

"Hmm. It never ceases to amaze me, that people have this thing that comes and goes on their arm, and no one ever really wonders about it.", Carl thought.

"Okay, so, you have a seat for me?"

"Yeah. United 137 to Bonn, you leave at 7:45 tonight from LaGuardia. Your boarding pass should be here in fifteen minutes or so. Did you remember everything this time?" Derek asked with a sideways smirk.

"Yes, I have everything this time, peckerhead." Carl shot back. "You got all the info on this doctor?"

"Of course! One of us around here actually *does* know what he's doing!" Now Derek was boasting.

"Yeah, too bad it's not you!"

Carl usually gave Derek a hard time, but he knew he never would have been able to do any of this without him.

He thought about the first time he met Derek Yosam. Carl was a service manager at a General Motors dealership in Manassas, Virginia and was in Pittsburg for a GM class on Dealer Management. It was warm so he had on a t-shirt. He had walked to this little tavern that everyone said had the best sandwiches in town. It looked kind of seedy, because it was so dark inside. Once his eyes adjusted though, it really was fairly nice. The bar looked like one giant piece of redwood, and the ceiling was that old timey stamped steel. Derek was the bartender.

"What can I get you?

"I'll try one of those pork tenderloin sandwiches and a New Castle, please."

"Comin' right up."

Derek headed off to the kitchen for the sandwich, and came back in what seemed like five seconds, with the food and beer.

"There you go. You wanna pay or run a tab, you're here for GM school right?" he asked.

"Yeah, but I'll go ahead and pay." Carl said.

"Okay", then Derek leaned over the bar some and looked at Carl's left arm with a very strange look on his face. Carl followed his gaze and noticed that the mark had risen and was a soft, burnt sienna color. He pulled his arm off the bar involuntarily.

"That's just a birthmark!" Carl exclaimed.

Derek leaned even farther over the bar and said very quietly, "That's strange, because I have one too, in exactly the same place." With that, Derek pulled up his shirt sleeve, and Carl saw the same square, brown, mark.

"Have you always had that?" asked Carl, quietly amazed.

"No, I got it when I was ten." replied Derek casually, "The aliens put it in me. When were you abducted?" Carl didn't know what to say, or think, for that matter. He had never met anyone else with the mark, much less anyone who thought they were abducted by aliens!

"I.....uhh...don't know." stammered Carl. "Umm...you think you were abducted by aliens?"

"Oh yeah, sure of it." Derek said matter-of-factly.

"What do you mean, sure of it?" Carl posed, still whispering.

"I'm sure of it. See, I remembered it all, even though you're not supposed to.

Also, I got pictures from inside the ship. You know, you're the first person I've met who's been through this, we need to talk more. I get off work about the same time your class ends, meet me here, and we'll go around the corner to my place. I'll show you some of the stuff I have, and the pictures." Derek trotted off to check on a couple of guys who came in and sat in a booth.

Carl's mind was reeling, his food was getting cold, and his beer getting hot. But, pictures of a ship? How could he?

More people started coming in and Derek was getting busy now with the lunch rush, so Carl tried to get his lunch down. The sandwich was as good as everyone had said, but he couldn't stop thinking about the things Derek had said, and the mark on his arm. This was too weird.

Carl finished up and left the money for the bill, and a tip, on the bar. On the way out Derek was at a table near the door and Carl said he'd be back later. Derek said he looked forward to it.

Carl walked back to the technical center and his class. The instructor didn't have a chance of getting Carl's attention. He couldn't get Derek and his claims out of his mind. He'd always toyed with the idea that the mark was something from an alien encounter, but never *really* thought it was. Not that he had any other ideas about it, but aliens?

The class let out at about three, and Carl walked back to the pub. Derek was already done work,

"You are one confused individual right about now, aren't you?" Derek asked with a grin, as they started to walk to Derek's apartment. "Umm, yeah, kinda." was all Carl could get out.

"Well, maybe I can clear things up for you. I'm just glad to finally run into someone else. I knew there were more people who'd been taken, besides all the flakes that say they have, but really haven't. Where are you from anyway?" Derek asked, as they walked up four steps to his door.

"Virginia.", answered Carl.

Derek opened the door, and they walked into what Carl thought was Doctor Frankenstien's original lab.

There were bottles and jars with electrodes in them, rows and rows of chemical bottles, all kinds of electronic gear, a huge Van Der Graaf generator, a dozen or more computers, and things that Carl couldn't even guess at what they were for. Derek explained that it had been a three story apartment building, but he bought it and gutted it, to make it into his workshop. Derek was an inventor.

"Well, what do you think?" he asked, once they were in far enough. "Ummmm, it's big." And it was. Derek really had gutted it, removed all the floors and walls so it was a three story shell about forty-five feet wide and a hundred and fifty feet long. He had reinforced the shell with huge I-beams.

"Yeah, I like a nice open feel to a place. Know what I mean?" Derek asked. "You want a beer?"

"Sure, why not."

Derek walked over to a large walk-in refrigerator and came back with a couple of cold Iron Cities.

"Okay, hey would you mind if I scan your arm before we get too into it here?" Derek asked Carl.

"Uhh, no…..scan for what?"

"I just want to make sure that thing in your arm's a chip like mine. I'm sure it is, but, you know. I made the scanner. It doesn't hurt or irradiate you, or anything.

"Hold still for a sec." Derek said as he ran a small, plastic bar over Carl's left forearm.

On one of the computer screens, Carl saw an image of what looked like any other computer chip appear. He figured it was a screensaver or something.   Derek turned to look at the screen and said, "I'll bet you've never seen that mark like that, have you? Of course, that's at 750 times magnification."

"What?!? That thing's in my arm? It really is a computer chip of some sort?" All of a sudden Carl felt a little woozy, this was all too much at once.

"Good thing you're sittin' man, you look like you're ready to fall out. Sit back and relax, and if you want, I'll tell you all I know about these things." Derek said.

"Sure" blurted Carl.

"Okay, well, the chip is actually this wonderful computer system, way more than a mere chip. It monitors every aspect of your body, and I mean everything.

10

It randomly monitors what you see, hear, smell, taste, feel, and think! It also monitors all of your vital stats.

"Did you ever feel like you were part of a machine, purring away in some corner?"

"Actually, umm……. yeah, sometimes." said Carl.

"Well, that's when it's monitoring. Then it saves all the data for later. It really is a most amazing little device." Derek went on, "But that's not all. The best part is what it does with the info. Remember in the bar how both of our marks were raised and brown?" he asked.

"Yeah." Carl looked at the mark on his arm, and noticed it was almost gone again.

"That's when it transmits the info it's gathered."

"Wha- wait, transmits it to who?" Carl asked with wonder.

"To the ship. It gets close enough to extract and read the data, from time to time. When the mark raises and changes color, it's like the antenna going up, and it sends the stored data."

This was too much for Carl and he passed

11

A couple of minutes later, when Carl awoke, Derek was sitting and looking at him.

"Sorry", Derek said, "I guess this is too much all at once for you. I'm just so used to all of this, I guess I never thought how it would affect other people."

"I'm having a pretty hard time believing this stuff." Carl admitted, "But, something in my head is telling me you're not making this up. What makes you think all of this stuff is going on?"

"Maybe I should start at the beginning. It may help you understand what's happening.

I was a gifted child. When I was five, I invented the digital camera.

When I was seven, I invented the magnetic drive engine. Between those two inventions, I was set for life. I invented a few other odd and ends before I was ten, when I had become the youngest millionaire in history.

Since then, I've invented hundreds of things, most of which no one even knows about. But suffice to say, I never need to work."

"What about the bar?" Carl asked.

"Oh, I own it. I always wanted to own a bar. But anyway, one of the things I invented when I was ten though, was a wireless digital micro camera. It was only three thousandths of an inch in diameter, about the thickness of a hair. I implanted it in my index fingernail, three days before I was abducted by the aliens. That's how I was able to take pictures inside the ship. I guess it was so small, they didn't catch it. Anyway, I think the pictures made it possible for me to remember what had happened on the ship.

They didn't really *do* that much. Most of the testing they did involved scanning technology. Except for implanting the chip. Even that wasn't bad. It was like getting a shot. A little tool on my arm and, pfft, it was done.

The funny thing is, the whole ordeal, from the time they took me, to when they put me back in my house, took less than five seconds. My folks never even missed me. So, I never told them about it.

I've spent my life since then, figuring out the chip and the travelling habits of the aliens.

I've tried a number of times to look for other people who've been through this, and have actually tracked down some people that have claimed to have been abducted, but they've all turned out to be fakes.

That's why I'm so thrilled to find you. I knew that someday, someone would come along who really had been taken like me."

"But I don't know that I've ever been abducted by aliens. If I have, I don't remember." Carl stressed.

"*You're not supposed to*." Derek said, "That's why I think the pictures are what allowed me to remember."

Carl couldn't think of a word to say. He thought he should just tell this whack-job it was nice to meet him, but he had to go. But still, he had that mark on his arm.

And what about those pictures, he wondered. "What about those pictures?" he thought aloud.

He instantly realized he had asked that question out loud, to which Derek jumped up and said, " Oh yeah, I'm certain you think I'm nuts, but I can assure you I'm not. Here look."

Derek clicked a mouse a couple of times and a picture folder came up on a monitor with pictures that looked like they were taken at a doctor's office. White walls, floor, ceiling. But oddly there were no windows, in fact, no anything else.

There were no chairs, lamps, lights in the ceiling, doors……nothing. The pictures were playing through in a slideshow.

All of a sudden, the camera moved, and what looked like some kind of being, came into view. Carl's jaw dropped and Derek paused the slideshow for a minute. "Cool huh?" Derek asked.

Carl was speechless.

Suddenly, the memory of his time on a ship like this, flooded his mind. The scans, the chip installation, the golden glow of the ship, the aliens, it all came back to him.Carl started to cry. Yes indeed, Carl's first meeting with Derek was interesting, to say the least.

Chapter 3

"Alright, here's your boarding pass and e-ticket."
Derek had brought Carl back from his memory
to the present. "If you want to crash for awhile,
I'll wake you up and take you to the airport."
Derek offered.

"Nah, I'm wired up now. I'll study up on the doc
and Bonn some. I can always get some sleep
on the plane. But I will hang around and let you
take me to the airport, thanks."

Carl sat down to his computer and got online.
First, he googled Bonn, to see where the good
doctor was in relation to the airport. Then he
checked out hotels and restaurants, etc. He
made a reservation at the Koninshoff hotel. It
was the best in Bonn.

He then got to the details on the good doctor
himself.

His name was Dr. Hans Von Bruchner. 52 years
old, a graduate of the Medical Academy of
Hamburg, and did his residence at the Giessen-
Justus-Liebig Universitatis hospital in Frankfurt.
He moved to Bonn and took up a general
practice. He seemed to be doing very well, was
married, and had a son and three grandchildren.

16

He was a certified abductee discovered eight years ago through the worldwide ad. This was his first find, and judging from the e-mails, he was pretty excited about it.

Carl always thought that doctors would be the best way to find people who don't believe the ad, or are afraid to investigate. Unfortunately, they didn't have anywhere near enough doctors in the ranks.

Ahh, the ad. "If you, or someone you know, thinks you/they, may have ever been abducted by aliens, call 856-535-6791 or e-mail chask@verizon.net or mail letter to Project Find Them; P.O. Box 2720; Edison, N.J. 08817."

What a fiasco! 43,762 calls, e-mails, and letters the first week. Luckily, Derek had developed some snazzy devices to handle all of the calls and e-mails, but that still left 6,000 plus letters to go through. But they knew the right questions to ask, and out of the first onslaught they actually came up with three legitimate abductees, which were certified and recruited, to help with the search.

The numbers did drop off after the first week, but the ad has been running in every newspaper in the world for fourteen years and still got plenty of hits, with proven recruits running about 1 in 650,000.

"So, any idea where the ship is today?" Carl asked getting up from his computer.

"No, no signal at all." replied Derek. That meant that it was out of range. Derek was working on an updated receiver to pick up the ship's signal when it was farther out in space, but right now they could only track it within 40,000 light-years or so, or about halfway across the Milky Way.

The new lab was a real marvel of technology. Of course Derek had final approval of all projects, since his money funded the whole thing, but a few of the brightest people on the planet had been recruited to work on the mission. The equipment that had been developed had landed Derek some 330 new patents, and plenty of government contracts.

A 265 picohertz transceiver could send and receive radio signals to the near edges of our galaxy, or, to put it in perspective, you could track a football's flight path fourteen million miles away! That was how Derek figured out where the ship was from.

Three years ago he finally got a fix on the ship by it's radio frequency and started to track it. He was limited as to how far away he could follow it, but luckily, Derek noticed it would stop for a long time at one point that was well within range. He decided that must be it's home port. The point was near Alnitak, in Orion's belt.

He got permission from the government to use the Hubbell to determine if there were planets around the star, and of course, there were. Four to be exact. He thought it was kind of interesting that it happened to be the third planet from the star, that was where the ship was based.

The next year, NASA secretly launched the AFFS, the Alnitak Fact-Finding Satellite. It was now one-quarter of the way there, only six more years to go, and maybe we would be able to contact the aliens, now called the Alnitaks, at their home.

"Okay, well I'm going to go visit Bonn to get a feel for it, then I may go ahead and take a little nap after all." Carl said.

"Allright." Derek barely responded.

Carl went to his module and settled in with some Bach and the sight and sound of Big Sur in the background.

This was another great invention of Derek's, the office module. Not to be confused with an office cubicle, the module was a sensory experience. Everything was

programmable to your tastes, desires, and /or needs. From lighting to scenery, from audio to olfactory, you could wake up in the Sarenghetti next to a pride of lions, and have lunch at an outdoor café in Paris. You could work at your desk overlooking the Mediterranean in Greece.

 Or you could travel to any place in the world and take a virtual tour.

The walls, ceiling, and floor, were seamless L.E.D. screens, covered with matte finish, unbreakable glass. Surround sound was provided by phase shifting, quartz speakers behind the screens. Aroma generators aroused your sense of smell. All programmed from the occupant's laptop. The furnishings were ergonomically designed for maximum comfort and efficiency.

Carl set an alarm for 4:30, he knew how easy it was to lose track of time in here, and punched in Bonn International Airport and started his journey. He entered the address for the hotel, rode there in a cab, and took a look around. Nice place, good choice, he thought, then he went to the doctor's office. It was a beautiful old brownstone. There was a brass plaque on the wall next to the door which read, "Bonne Musique Conservitats". Then

he took some time to walk the streets and look around. Bonn was a very nice city. Clean, lots of flowers, and neatly trimmed lawns.

It was only 1:30, so he decided he would take a nap for a while. He left the music and the sound of the surf on, laid down, and fell asleep about the same time his head hit the pillow.

It seemed like ten seconds later when his alarm woke him. As soon as his head cleared a little, he knew that he'd gotten a good rest. He felt great.

He left his module and went out into the lab. Mark Craig, one of the volunteers, was studying something on a computer. He was a communications specialist, so Carl figured he was working on new frequency generators or some such thing.

"Derek still around?" Carl asked Mark.

"He went over to Nellie's to grab a bite. Call him on his cell if you're hungry. He's bringing some food back for me and Sandy. She's in the astro lab working on some tracking paths."

"Nah, I'll eat on the plane. It'll be a dinner flight. I think I'll go see what Sandy's up to though." said Carl.

Sandy Ballard was a 28 year-old, big-boobed, redhead, astro-physicist. She was already well known for some of her bigger discoveries, including the now standard method of finding black holes. She'd written five books, and was the head of the astrophysics department at M.I.T.

She and Carl had dated a few times, and always enjoyed each other's company, so it was no surprise when Carl came up behind her and kissed her neck.

"I know you're heading out in a couple of hours, so don't start anything you don't have time to finish!" scolded Sandy sarcastically.

"Okay, not that I wouldn't rather stay here and spend the night with you." Carl sulked.

"Hey, you always know where I'm at. Here or at school. All you have to do is pry yourself away from your beloved mountains." She was enjoying giving him a hard time.

"You've been to the house, and you've said you love it. I still can't figure out why you don't move down to Virginia with me." Carl did know though, of course.

"Because I'm not commuting to Edison, or Boston, from Virginia. That's why, and you know it!"

They'd had this discussion many times, and Carl knew it was time to change the subject.

"Have you found any new trajectories for anything?" he asked almost innocently.

"You think you can change the subject that easily?" Now she was mocking him. But he didn't mind. He wondered if he was coming to love her. She really was beautiful and very sweet. She would kill him with sex though, if he let her. But he thought that it would be a great way to go.

"Well, I have to try." he said sheepishly.

She laughed, and so did he. She told him that nothing new had come up yet, and asked where he was going this time.

"Bonn, Germany." he said.

"Ohhh, I like Bonn. I was there twice for award presentations. It's a very nice city. Where are you staying?"

"The Koninshoff."

"Ooohh, I've never stayed there, but it's supposed to be really nice. A couple of blocks from there, I think, is Kiergstadt Gardens. They're beautiful all year long, and they have a great restaurant. Make sure you check it out."

"I will" he said, "I better start getting my stuff together for this trip, I guess. See you when I get back?"

"Somewhere along the line I suppose. You know me, back and forth. Have a good one and be safe." She gave him a kiss and hug, then he left.

I really should marry that girl someday, he thought. But, then again, as usual, he thought about how young she was, and how old he was.

When he got back to the lab, Derek was back with food, and was on his way to take Sandy her sandwich.

"This is Sandy's, you wanna take it down to her?" he asked Carl.

"No, that's okay, I just left her."

"Oh, okay. Well there's a cheesesteak, extra cheese, lettuce, and mayo for you. I know you probably figured on eating on the plane, but I also know you can't resist Nellie's cheesesteaks, since you can't get them in Jerkwater, Virginia" his voice drifting off as he went down the long hallway to the astro lab.

Well, he was right about that. There were a couple of acceptable steak joints near his home, but they weren't Nellie's.

Sandy had decided to take a break and come up to the main lab and eat. They were all sitting around slinging the bull and eating, when a small alert went off on Derek's computer.

"Ha, they're back!" he squealed. "I knew it would be today!"

He jumped to his computer, punched the mouse a couple of times, and they all watched on the big screen as the tracking info started scrolling through.

"They're coming into the galaxy near Sagittarius!"

Derek was like a kid at Christmas every time the alien ship came into range of his trackers.

"Sandy, can you check the trajectory, please? Looks like they may be heading home." Derek asked.

Sandy went to a work station and plugged the tracking information into her projection program, and said,"

Yessiree, they're heading home to Alnitak."

They all watched as this alien ship sped through space at near the speed of light, and arrived home, a quarter of the way across the Milky Way, in less than two minutes. It still amazed all of them, every time they watched.

"I just can't wrap my head around going that fast." said Carl. "How *do* they keep from running into asteroids and moons, and planets, and all the other junk out in space?"

Derek shook his head, "I wish I knew." he said

Carl had survived the security checks, and the plane had lifted off. He got comfortable for the eight hour flight, pulled out his laptop, and ordered a beer. He looked out of the window and already New York City was growing small and distant. Carl wasn't afraid to fly, on the contrary, he loved it, but he did always wonder if he would live through the flight.

He played some online games, checked out Kiergstadt Gardens, and the restaurant, and sent an e-mail back to the lab, just to let everybody know the plane made it into the sky uneventfully. It was pretty rare these days for any flight to take off without some kind of problem or delay.

"Friggin' terrorists", he thought. "All the crap we all have to go through cause of these radicals."

The stewardess came by to check on him, and he asked for a pillow. He decided he might as well get some more rest. The stewardess came back with two pillows, she said they were a little thin, and dimmed his overhead light for him. He thanked her and fell asleep in no time.

Carl awoke with a start. He had been dreaming he was driving next to a cliff and lost control. He had just crashed through the guardrail when he woke up.

He looked at his watch when he regained his composure. It was ten after three.

He was thirsty. He headed toward the front of the plane to see if anyone was awake. The pretty young stewardess was sitting in her jump seat sleeping. Carl was getting a water from the self serve bar, when she woke up. She apologized for not hearing his page, and he explained that he hadn't paged her. He didn't want to bother her in case she was sleeping. She looked at her watch and said she had to get started preparing for landing anyway, and thanked him for being so nice. He said it was nothing, and went back to his seat.

He looked out of the window and this time he saw what he knew was the west coast of Scotland and it was dawn. Yeah, we'll be landing in an hour, or so, and let's see, Scotland, four hours ahead, so it's after seven. He pulled out the laptop again and checked the weather in Bonn. Clear and cool. Temps in the low forties, with a chance of showers this afternoon. He figured he would change his jacket when he got to the airport, but it would be a quick cab ride to the hotel, so he decided he would just wait.

A while later, he was hailing a cab in front of the airport.

"Guten-tag. Hotel Koninshoff." he told the cabbie.

The cabbie spoke English and asked if he was in Bonn for business or pleasure.

Carl told him pleasure. The cabbie said to check out Kiergstadt Gardens while he was in town. Carl said he'd think about it.

When Carl got to the hotel, he found that they had given him the Kurt Masur suite on the fourth floor. The room was named after the great conductor. It looked out over a beautiful Rhine. Past that was the Drachenfels and the Siebengebirge mountains. The room was lovely. A sitting room with satellite tv, very cushy couch and chair, a wet bar, and a desk for working. It was decorated with pictures of Beethoven by local artist, Ralf Klose. The bedroom had a king bed, another overstuffed chair, and an antique armoire that had a small plaque stating that it had come from a fifteenth century castle in Brussels.

The bathroom was huge, with a shower/sauna, garden tub, double sinks, and a dressing area.

He dropped all of his gear inside the door and sat down to

call the doctor. He wanted to let him know he was in town,

and set up an appointment to visit with him. Before he could dial the phone though, there was a knock on the door. He looked through the peephole and saw a beautiful blond girl.

He opened the door and the girl introduced herself as Gretchen. She explained that she was the hotel concierge and welcomed him. She gave him her card and asked if there was anything she could get for him.

She told him to keep in mind, that many things that were illegal in the U.S., were not here. And that she could get him almost *anything* he could want. He thanked her and said he would remember that. He asked her if she could get him a ticket to visit Kiergstadt Gardens. She said it would be waiting at the front desk whenever he was ready to go. He thanked her again and she left.

He finally pulled out his cell phone to call Dr. Bruchner, but realized it was only nine thirty in the morning. He remembered reading in the doctor's profile, that his office

hours were 10 a.m. to 5 p.m. He decided to get
a shower

and change clothes. He sat in the sauna for
about twenty minutes, then took a nice hot
shower. He walked through the suite naked and
took his clothes into the bedroom. He put stuff
in drawers, and hung up what needed to be, in
the antique armoire. He put on a pair of grey
slacks and a black and white pullover.

He went downstairs to check out the hotel
restaurant, the Oliveto, an Italian restaurant that
also catered to international tastes.

He decided to get some breakfast before he
started his day. He saw Gretchen again when
he entered the lobby.

She greeted him by name and escorted him to
the restaurant. She told him that breakfast and
lunch were on the house during his stay and
dinners and drinks were very reasonable. She
also said she already had his Garden ticket at
the front desk, and to call her if he needed
anything else.

He was starting to notice just how pretty she
was. He also wondered just what she would do,
to make his stay

enjoyable. Oh well, it was then that he realized he hadn't

eaten since the cheesesteak yesterday. He sat down in a corner booth, and after perusing the menu, decided on an early lunch instead. He ordered Pasta Aoste Valley. This was pasta with White Lardo bacon and a warm corn fritter, and a coffee. He called the doctor while he was waiting for his food.

He had forgotten about the strange ringtones in Germany, even on cellphones.

"Guten-tag! Dies ist Dr. Hans Von Bruchner. Wie kahn ich Ihenen helfer?"

"Guten-tag, Herr doctor, sprechen zie Anglais?" Carl asked in his best German.

"Yes, who is calling please?"

"It's Carl Haskins doctor, from Project Find Them."

"Ahh, Mr. Haskins. I've been waiting for your call. Have you made it to Bonn okay?"

"Yes sir. My trip was fine. I'm at the Hotel Koninshoff, I'm going to have some lunch, could we meet this afternoon, by any chance?" Carl asked, anxious to meet him.

"I'm sorry", the doctor said, "I have to go to Munich to assist in a very serious surgery today. It's a reconstruction and multiple organ transplant. It involves a lot of people. If I could get out of it, I would, but…"

"Oh, no, that's okay. When do you expect to return?"

"I should be back tomorrow morning around eight. I hope to be back in my office for opening at ten. Why don't you come by at noon tomorrow. We can have lunch and talk. Do you know where my office is?" he asked.

"Yes" said Carl, "I'll see you tomorrow then. Good luck with the surgery."

"Thank you. The patient is actually an American girl that was badly burned in a fire.

We are transplanting three organs to try to give her a little more normal life. I'll see you tomorrow then, goodbye."

"Good bye doctor."

It was perfect timing. As soon as he put his cell phone away, his lunch arrived. So, he thought, while he ate a wonderful meal, the whole day to myself. I guess I might as well go see these gardens everyone's talking about.

He stopped by the front desk, and got his ticket, then walked the two blocks to a huge arch made entirely of roses. "Kiergstadt Gardens" in the arch, was made of orange rose blossoms. He wondered how they kept the roses so fresh looking in November. He passed under the arch and followed a walkway to the admission gate. He handed over his ticket and got a map of the garden, menu for the restaurant, and a package of dried rose petals as a souvenir. Maybe I'll give these to Sandy when I get back, he thought. He walked through the gardens and understood why everybody made such a fuss. It was pretty incredible, and big. There were over a hundred topiaries. The biggest was a fifty-five foot tall giraffe. He had looked at the map, and read that the garden sits on twenty-two acres in the middle of town.

The land was donated to the city by Premier Vogelzand in 1534, to be used exclusively for the finest botanical garden in the country. And it had been ever since.

By the time he got through the garden, it was after four. He was in front of the Garden Restaurant. Well, he thought, if this is as good as the garden was, it should be great.

It was! It was actually more like a beer garden, with the flowers and other flora everywhere. There were four long tables down through the hall that had to have been 150 yards long. There were probably 1,500 people eating. The food and the beer never stopped, and he was pretty well wiped when he finally left, at about nine.

He made his way back to the hotel, which he was glad was only two blocks away, went to his room and flopped on the bed. He woke up about one in the morning, tired, but feeling okay. He got undressed, set his alarm for seven, and went out like a light.

Chapter 5

Carl woke up at seven, took a shower, got
dressed and went to breakfast. Gretchen was at
her concierge desk, and he asked if she could
have a cab waiting for him at eleven.

"Of course." she said "How did you like the
Garden?"

"It was wonderful, for sure. Although, I'm not
sure how much I remember after dinner. I had a
few beers more than I should have, maybe." he
chuckled.

"Ach, but that's what it's there for, to enjoy."

"Well I sure did, thanks. See you later."

"Goodbye."

Carl had a nice breakfast, bought a Washington
Post at the gift shop, and went back to his room.
He wanted to get his gear ready, just in case
they could get this girl to come to the doctor's
office today. He wanted to get the testing done
and get home. As nice as Bonn was, he always
wanted to get back from these trips.

There had been over a thousand now, and the novelty of traveling the world had worn off long ago.

He had been to some interesting places though. Places where you don't find tourists very often. A Bedouin camp in the Sahara, a village of pygmies in Brazil, an outpost in Antarctica. Crazy where they would find these people, but, where they are, is where they are. The only reason he still went on the trips, is because he loved seeing the people's faces when they remember. When he tells them why he's there to see them, they all look at him like he's nuts. A perfectly natural reaction. Then he shows them his chip, and they start wondering. If the ship happens to be near, and the chips are swollen and brown, then they really get intrigued. Then, he shows them the pictures, and with every single one so far, at the first picture of the alien, they remember. It's been the same with all 2,067. Then they remember it all, just like Carl had, so many years ago at Derek's place in Pittsburg. At ten till eleven, Carl headed down to meet his cab, his roller bag in tow.

About five minutes later, a cab pulled up. The driver put down his window and asked him "Haskins?"

"Yes." said Carl

He hoisted his bag onto the back seat, got in and told the driver "221 Vigel Strassen, please."

This cabbie was quiet, which Carl didn't mind at all.

He didn't have to think up any stories to tell him if he asked what he was doing.

He leaned back and wondered again if they would be able to get the girl to come into the office.

After about a twenty minute ride they pulled up to the old "Bonne Musique Conservitats" building. The fare was four euros and twenty. Carl gave him a fiver and wished him Guten-naben.

He walked up the steps and twisted the bell in the middle of the door. A middle aged woman opened the door and asked "Mr. Haskins?" When Carl answered that it was he, she led him into a small waiting room. A couple of minutes later Dr. Bruchner came in.

"Guten-naben, I'm so glad to finally meet you. You were one of the original founders of the project weren't you?" he asked.

"Yes, that's right." Carl said.

"Please, come into my study. I have a couple of odds and ends to take care of, then we can go to lunch."

"Thank you."

The doctor led Carl to a gorgeous study with four tall windows on the south wall. The rest of the walls were covered with floor-to-ceiling bookshelves.

"I won't be ten minutes." said the doc.

"No hurry." Carl assured him.

While the doctor was finishing his business, Carl decided to check out his library.

A very educated fellow, judging by his collection, Carl thought. He had books from all over the world, in all languages and genres.

In about twenty minutes, the doctor came back in, apologized for taking so long, and led Carl out of the house and down the street to a little restaurant called "Liepzig's".

It was a traditional German restaurant. Carl ordered saur-braten and the doctor got swinebrunner. They both got a Dinkel-Aaken.

"I was very excited when I saw the mark on the girl. She is my first find." the doctor said.

"Yes, I know. Congratulations, and thank you for the call. Is the girl local?" Carl asked.

"Yes. She lives on the Vierschtigstratten on the other side of the river."

"Do you think we could get her to come by your office today." Carl asked.

"I don't know. What would I tell her to make her come?"

"You can be honest. Tell her you'd like a specialist to look at that mark on her arm, and that the top guy is in town just for today." Carl was setting up the doctor, and he didn't even realize it.

"Ach du Liebre! I don't know why I didn't think of that. Tsk. So simple. We'll call her as soon as we get back to my office. How many people have you found now?" he asked.

"Two-thousand & sixty-seven. Your girl will be sixty-eight, if she's proves to be one of us."

"Do you think there are a lot more?"

"Don't know, we don't get tips like we used to, but we still get them. We just keep checking them out."

"And how do you like Bonn, and the Koninshoff?"

The doc raised his bushy eyebrows when he said the name of the hotel. "You know that's the premiere hotel in Bonn, don't you?"

"Yes," Carl chuckled, "I always travel first class. It's one of the benefits of being a senior member of a privately-funded organization."

They finished up their lunches and headed back to Dr. Bruchner's office. He had his secretary pull the girl's information card as they went back to his study.

"Ahh, here we are. Coorda Harflutz, let's see if I can reach her." He dialed her number, but there was no answer. He tried her cell number, and she answered.

He asked if she could make it round to his office and why, and she said she could come around three. That's when she got done work. The doc said that would be fine and he would expect her.

Carl said he would go and let the doctor get back to work, and asked if he could leave his bag.

"That's fine, but you're welcome to stay, if you like." said Bruchner.

"I saw the Liegensfelter Museum down the street, so I thought I would check it out. I'll be back around 2:30."

Carl enjoyed the walk to the museum, only three blocks away, almost as much as he enjoyed the museum itself. He had always loved how old everything was in Europe. Ancient architecture, ancient relics, and ancient history. America was so new, comparatively. The museum was nice. It had some neat stuff, including the German crown jewels. This was actually the royal museum from the days when kings ruled Germany, so it was a little different from what Carl had expected. Luckily, it was a small museum, as Carl didn't have a lot of time.

He headed back to the doctor's office and arrived at about twenty till three. The doctor was in his study, and Carl asked if there was a room he would bring Coorda into, and if he could set up his equipment in there. Bruchner showed him to an examination room, and Carl set up his laptop, camera, scanner, and a small digital voice recorder to tape the conversation. Then they waited.

Coorda Harflutz showed up at ten after three. The doctor brought her into the exam room and introduced her to Carl, and let Carl take over from there. Luckily for him, she spoke perfect English.

"Good afternoon, Coorda. The doctor contacted me when he discovered the little mark on your arm. I need to ask you a few questions, and do a couple of tests.

Also, I would like to record our entire visit for accuracy in paperwork later.

Is that okay with you?"

"Yes, I guess so." she said, "But what's the big deal about this mark? My last doctor said it was just a mole. Is it a sign of cancer or something?"

"No,no. I'm sorry if this has alarmed you. It's not a health risk of any kind. But I will explain all of this as we go along."Carl assured her. "May I start?" he asked.

"Okay."she said, perhaps a little reluctantly.

Carl started the recorder and the questions.

"Allright, could you please say your name, age, address, and the date please."

"Coorda Harflutz, 35 years, 4317 Vierschtigstratten; Bonn, Germany. Today is 3 November, 2013."

"Now Coorda, the doctor told me when you came in, you mentioned having strange dreams. Is that right?"

"Yes, it's very strange. I know I'm having these dreams, but when I wake up, I can't remember a thing about them." Coorda looked frustrated.

"Okay Coorda, thank you. Now, this little mark on your arm, how long has it been there, do you think."

"I don't know, a long time I suppose. I don't seem to remember it being there when I was real little, but I know it was there when I was a teenager."

"Okay, very good. Does it ever hurt you, or does it ever change appearance?"

"Well it never hurts, although it does change at times. That's the only time I really notice it."

"And how does it change, can you tell me?"

"It raises up a little. Most of the time I don't pay attention to it, because I can't see it, and it's flat. But other times, it raises up and turns a brown color."

" How often does this happen, would you say. And, how long does it stay in this raised state?"

"Not very often. Sometimes it won't do it for a couple of years, sometimes two or three times in a few months. And the same with how long it stays. Usually not long, a few minutes maybe. There were a couple of times though, when it seems like it was up for a few days. What does it mean doctor?"

Carl gave a small, but compassionate chuckle. "I'm not actually a doctor," Carl told her, "I'm a researcher. It's time for me to do a test on th mark now. It won't hurt you at all, and only takes a second, then I will start to explain all of this to you, okay?"

Coorda agreed.

Coorda, was a computer architect. She graduated Summa Cum Laude from California Polytech in 1999, and was now a head Computer Architect for Apple Ind.;Germany.

Carl ran the scanner over Coorda's left arm, and the image of the chip appeared on the screen within a couple of seconds. He had turned the laptop so Coorda could see it.

She looked at the screen not sure of what she was looking at, until Carl told her.

"Okay Coorda, you have to be strong here, because I'm about to tell you some strange things. That picture is a three-d image of what's in your arm, it is a computer, and it's probably been there since you were ten years old."

"What is a computer doing in my arm, and how do you know when it got there? Who are you, what's this all about?" Coorda was getting a little alarmed.

"It's okay Coorda, please try to stay calm, I told you I'd explain all of this, and I will. I just have a

 certain way we have to do this, because it's quite remarkable really. You're number two-thousand sixty-eight in a select group of people on this planet that have these chips, that we know of, so far. The doctor and myself included. I tell you this so that you know you are in the company of two people who have been exactly where you are right now. What I'm about to tell you, you'll find unbelievable, but I promise, it's all true. Okay? May I continue?"

This is always the point where Carl had to be at his best. The last thing you want is someone bolting out into the streets, yelling about alien attacks or something.

"Okay."said Coorda.

"Allright, when you were around ten years old, which is the age all of us had this experience, you were taken aboard an alien ship. They didn't hurt you, but they did implant this chip."

Carl gave Coorda a few seconds to absorb this. Then he continued, "This chip is a monitor and a transmitter. When it rises up and changes color, it's sending your information to an alien spaceship. Do you understand, Coorda?"

"Uh...sure. I was taken on a spaceship and they implanted this thing in my arm, and now they come by once in a while to read the data. Okay." She had the typical look on her face that everyone has at this point , which says, "Call the nuthouse, this guy's crazy as a loon!"

"That's right. Okay, now, I know you think I'm nuts, but I'd like to continue and show you some pictures, okay?"

"Sure, why not." she said.

"Carl adjusted the laptop's position so it was directly facing Coorda, and started the slideshow. She saw pictures of what looked like a very bright white doctor's office, although it was strangely devoid of doors, windows, etc. She watched with near indifference.

Then the camera moved to a being. Carl paused the slideshow so Coorda could absorb the picture. She was mesmerized, then she remembered it all. And she started to cry.

Carl moved to hold her and assured her it was okay, they had all reacted the same way. Everyone had, who had been through it.

2,068.

They talked for a while, Carl explained the Project, and asked if she would be willing to help in the search.

47

She said she would do what she could. Carl gave her the contact information for the Project and Derek, then, the interview was over.

Chapter 6

"How'd it go?" Derek asked before Carl even got through the gate. "Is she certified? Is she going to help?"

"Yes, and yes. She'll be sending an e-mail, if she hasn't already. She can be a huge help with Mac users. She's a computer architect with Apple. She thought the whole thing was pretty neat once she got over the shock."

"Good, we can always use more computer people, especially Mac qualified. How'd you like Bonn?"

"It's a nice city. They sure do like their brewskis. I got pasted at a beer garden the other night. But it was cool. I'm just glad to be back, and I'll be even happier when I can get back to my mountain."

"You're not going back tonight are you?" Derek asked. He never liked it when Carl would head off for Virginia in the middle of the night.

"No, I didn't really sleep that great at the hotel, and I couldn't sleep at all on the plane. There was a woman with a baby on board.

49

That kid cried the entire flight until twenty minutes or so before we landed. Little shit. So, no

I'll crash at the lab and head out in the morning. Umm....Sandy isn't, by any chance, around, is she?" Carl asked a little too hopefully.

"Sorry bud, but no, she went back to school this morning. And what do you care, you're tired, remember?" Derek laughed.

"I wouldn't be if she was at the lab. Although I'd probably still fall asleep!" now Carl laughed.

The next morning, Carl hopped into his Suburban and headed south towards Virginia. Carl, as Sandy had said, did love his mountains. He lived right on top of a mountain between Winchester and Front Royal. To the West, he could see up, down, and across the Shenandoah Valley. To the East he could see almost to D.C. He wondered what he would be doing, and where he'd be living if he hadn't met Derek. Ten years ago, Derek had told him that he needed his top investigator and project manager to have a place where he could really unwind. When Carl found this place he didn't think Derek would seriously buy it for him, but he did.

It was late afternoon. Carl lit a fire in the woodstove, opened the curtains, grabbed a beer from the fridge, took off his clothes, and sat down in his favorite chair to watch the sun set.

Carl was a nudist, which was another benefit of this house, no neighbors.   Ahhh, home again, home again, jiggety-jig!

Carl woke up around 7:30, he had missed the sunset. Oh well. He looked at the thermometer, sixty-four. The above average temperatures were still holding. He slid open the glass door and went out onto the wraparound deck, and looked up. Another thing he loved about his house, a billion stars were his only neighbors.

"Hello Orion, and Alnitaks." he said aloud. He raised his now warm beer to them. He had always greeted Orion when he saw him in the sky. It meant so much more now though, knowing that somewhere around the easternmost star in his belt, was a world full of beings that sped around space, like people here speed around highways.

He walked around the house on the deck, drank his beer, and decided he might as well do some work. He went back in, threw a couple of sticks on the fire, and sat down at his computer. Check e-mail, bunch of spam in the folder, nothing interesting, delete. An e-mail from Gretchen Kiersdorf.

Thank you for staying at the Koninshoff, hope you enjoyed your stay, blah, blah, blah. One from Derek, another hit on the ad, in Ohio, investigator en route. Sounds like it may be a real one. Horizon Wireless, your online bill is ready to be viewed. That was it for mail.

Start the report for Coorda.

His phone rang. It was Derek.

"Yes?"

"Hey, sorry for calling, I know you just got home, but something's happening. Something I've never seen." said Derek.

The tone of his voice made Carl sit up straight. "What Derek?"he asked.

It took Derek a couple of seconds before he could get it out. "The ship is here." Derek waited.

"Carl? Did you hear me?"

It took Carl about ten seconds for it to sink in. "Yeah, I heard you. Where exactly is it? Is it like 'here', on the ground, 'here' in orbit over us, or 'here' in our solar system?" Carl wanted details, but didn't really.

"It's in orbit, technically. It's parked behind the moon, and staying there." said Derek. "I've been waiting for this day for so long, but now that it's here, I kinda wish it would go away.

"Who else knows about it?" Carl wanted to know.

"Well, I haven't gotten a call from NASA or Department of Defense yet, so I guess you and me are the only ones, at this point anyway. There's nobody else here at the lab."

"I wonder why now?" Carl posed.

"I don't know, what the hell's going to happen when somebody else does figure out it's there? What if defense tries to attack it? Who knows what these things can do? They might blow up our planet or something." Derek was starting to rant a little.

"I don't think so." said Carl, "If they were going to do that, they would have already, most likely." Carl was doing his best to reassure his friend, but it wasn't really working, for either of them.

"Can you come back up tomorrow?" Derek asked.

"Yeah, let me get a few hours sleep. I'll be there as soon as I can. Call me if anything else develops."

"Okay, sorry again buddy, but you know me, chickenshit first class!"

"Hey, don't worry about it. I'll see you in the a.m."

"Thanks. See ya." And Derek hung up.

Carl wondered if he was really going to be able to sleep.

He thought he had to try. It had been a busy few days, and he was wiped out. He threw two more logs on the fire and banked it back. He pulled open his futon and turned out his work lamp. He left the drapes open and fell asleep looking at the stars.

When he woke up, it was just after two. Carl got up, peed, checked the fire, and laid back down. Next time he woke it was ten till four. This time he was awake.

He got up, threw some fresh clothes in his bag, packed the laptop, grabbed a Red Bull, and headed out into a brisk morning for the drive back to Edison.

Chapter 7

It was almost 10:30 when Carl walked into the lab to find Derek staring at a monitor.

"Still there?" he asked.

"Yeah." Derek turned and Carl could see he'd been looking at the screen all night. His eyes looked like they were bleeding.

"You look like crap, my friend" said Carl.

"Thanks."

"Tell me what to look at, and I'll keep watch for a while. You go get some sleep." offered Carl.

"Sleep!? You think I can sleep!? What if it turns out I've caused the end of the world with all this stuff? How do you think I can sleep?!?" Derek was almost crazed, his eyes were wild, and he was almost panting.

"Derek, nothing like that is going to happen. And even if they come and zap us all, number one, it wouldn't be your fault, and number two, we'll probably all die anyway, so who cares?!" Carl didn't know if this would help or not, but he had to try something.

55

All of a sudden the chips in their arms felt like they were being ripped out. They looked at the chips, wide-eyed. They were over a half inch above their arms and were glowing bright red. They looked at the monitor.

Derek said "They're right over us, one-hundred feet over us."

"What the…….." was all Carl got out.

Chapter 8

Carl came to in a stark white room, and promptly realized where he was. He passed out.

The next time he awoke, he was seated in a room with a dim golden glow, in a very comfortable chair. As his eyes adjusted to the light, he noticed Derek in a chair next to him. He was still out.

Carl looked around and saw a raised gallery in front of them, and a podium. He couldn't believe he was on the ship, but it had to be. What had happened, he wondered.

Right then, Derek started to wake up. He jumped as he came to in strange surroundings. Then he noticed Carl looking at him, and he felt some relief, but not much. He didn't have a good feeling about this.

"How long have you been awake?" he whispered to Carl.

"Just a few minutes. I woke up earlier in the white room, but only for a second. When I recognized it, I guess I passed out. Then I woke up here."

"I've always wanted to get back on this ship, but now that I'm here, I don't think I like it. I'm afraid Carl. What if we've pissed these people, things, whatever they are, off?"

"Let's not flip ourselves out yet. Maybe they just decided to finally make contact with us, to be friends." Again, he tried to be reassuring for his friend, but again, it wasn't helping either of them at all.

Carl was scared too.

Then four beings entered the room from what seemed like nowhere. There was no sound. No opening doors, no nothing. They were just there.

Carl was in awe. Derek was frozen in his chair.

The four beings hovered in the gallery, looking at them without a sound.

They were so oddly beautiful. They were very tall, better than seven feet. Their skin, for lack of a better term, was a softly glowing gold color. It was like there was a light inside them. They had, what looked like eyes, that were a different shade of gold, and glowed brighter than their skin. There were no other features on their faces. No mouth or nose, no ears or hair, but somehow they were still quite beautiful.

Carl couldn't see any legs or arms, but he thought maybe it was just too dark.

One of them glided to the podium. Then, out of the air came the question, "Why have you attacked us?" It was kind of like the voice was in Carl and Derek's heads. It was very disconcerting.

Carl and Derek couldn't tell if it was talking, or using mental telepathy, or what exactly. This isn't good, thought Derek. We have pissed them off. Damn!

But Carl spoke up, calm as a cucumber. "To my knowledge, we haven't attacked you. If you feel that we have, I apologize for all the people of Earth."

There was a long silence, then, "We intercepted and disarmed the weapon you sent at us, two of your Earth years ago."

"Oh, that wasn't a weapon. It was an information gathering probe. We just wanted to see what you and your home were like, we wanted to see if we could contact you." said Carl.

Derek meanwhile, was in shock. He couldn't believe any of this and thought sure he must be dreaming. How did they know English? How were they talking? Who the hell were they? Why did they capture him and Carl? Why them?

He decided it was time for him to start asking the questions here.

"Why did you bring us here, now?" asked Derek in a defiant tone.

"Because of all the people on your planet, we know that you two are the engineers of the plan to attack us." said the alien.

"What makes you think we want to attack you?" Carl wailed, "You couldn't be more wrong about our intentions!"

The alien explained, "We've been watching your world for 20,000 years. We know how your race conducts itself. You destroy everything. It's just how you are." It then added icily, "That's why you need to be stopped."

The aliens, however they did it, had mastered inflection and tone of the English language. Which is why the alien's last statement sent a shudder through both Carl and Derek.

"What do you mean, we need to be stopped?' Carl asked.

"You have figured out space travel, you have found us, you will find others in the universe. You will, if left on your own, destroy all that you find. It's what you do at this point in your evolution. That's why you must be stopped now."

"Others?" asked Derek. "How many others?"

"There are millions of inhabited worlds in the universe. Many have evolved past their destructive phases, and live peacefully with the rest of the universe. Others, like your world, have not. Still others are very early in their evolution and won't be a threat for thousands or millions of years. But your world is now the most dangerous threat to universal peace, so you will be stopped."

"So, what, you're going to blow our planet up, or something?" Now Carl was getting defiant.

"Certainly not! This is why you're so dangerous. You don't yet understand the theory of universal peace, because you don't know it. This is not your people's fault. All civilizations go through it. Our own world was quarantined six million Earth years ago. It took us almost seven-thousand years before we could conform to the Universal Code. It may take Earth more, or less time. Every civilization is different. But you will be quarantined. It has already been decided by the Counsel. That is why you two were summoned. You must tell the leaders of your world what is going to happen."

The alien stopped long enough for all of this to sink into Carl and Derek's minds.

He then continued "In the Universal Code, there is no destruction of anything, at any time. The penalties for breaking the code are harsh, but also non-destructive.

During your stay with us you will receive the teachings of The Code by tutors assigned to teach you, then you will teach your people how to live in true peace. First on your own planet, then how to live peacefully in the Universe. When your planet's training is complete, you'll be tested, and if you pass the test, the quarantine will be lifted and you'll be taught the science required to travel in the universe, and meet the rest of it's inhabitants."

"How do you propose to quarantine a whole planet?" Carl broke in.

"An unbreakable force field will be placed around your planet. Your attempts at space travel will end. The field will be placed at the edge of your atmosphere. And will stay there until your training is complete and all testing passed."

"How are we supposed to convince the world that the aliens have put a force field around us. No one will believe us." Derek said.

"We are going to teach you how to convince your society of our presence. We will also give you some tokens to prove that you have met us.

But ultimately, most societies don't believe the emissaries.

That's why they probably won't believe you until they launch a few spaceships and they're destroyed."

"I thought you said you weren't allowed to destroy stuff?" Carl fired at the alien.

"You're not listening, we won't destroy anything. Your own people will. That's their way. But they will realize eventually that you are telling the truth. Then the training will begin on your planet." it said.

Carl and Derek sat in their chairs. They looked at the aliens and tried to think of something else to say.

But there were so many questions, at this point, neither of them knew where to start.

Finally Carl asked, "What do we do next?"

"We begin your training. We will teach you what you need to know about us, and the rest of the universe, so that you can pass the information on to your planets best minds. We will also teach you how to perform mind sway, which is a method of making other beings see your point of view more easily.

But first, we will give you the tokens you will take back with you."

Two small plates, about the size of a deck of cards, lifted from the podium and moved to Carl and Derek. They hung in the air in front of them until both men grabbed them.

These things were wonderful. They were warm, and cool. They were light, and heavy. They were all the colors of the rainbow, yet you could see right through them. Carl and Derek had never seen anything like them.

The being that had been 'talking' to them, moved back to the other three. Another being moved to the podium.

"You may call me Ther-Leh. We are of the race called Gilfeng.

I am charged with your training, my staff and I will teach you what you need to know, to convince your people of our presence. I'm sure you have a lot of questions, but first I will take you to your quarters. Follow me."

Carl and Derek got out of their chairs to follow Ther-Leh, until he went through the wall of the room. They, of course, stopped. Ther-Leh came back and urged them to follow. They told him they couldn't walk through walls.

He assured them that they could, if they forgot everything they knew while on this ship, and just do as Ther-Leh says.

He turned and went through the wall again. Carl and Derek looked at each other, and stepped off through the wall to find Ther-Leh facing them.

"See?"

They were in a dimly lit corridor, thirty or forty feet wide, and they couldn't see either end. There were hundreds of Gilfeng in the corridor.

They were going in all directions, passing through walls, the floor, the ceiling. It was the most bizarre thing either of them had ever seen. They could tell now, that the Gilfeng didn't have any appendages. They simply blended into the ship. It was quite strange to see.

They had walked probably seventy or eighty feet when Ther-Leh turned left and went through the wall of the corridor. They followed with only slightly less hesitation than the first time. They really didn't know if they would ever get used to this.

On the other side of the wall was a room, actually a suite of rooms. It looked like the nicest five-star hotel either of them had ever seen.

There was Louis XVI furniture, a full wet bar, a table bursting with all kinds of food, hot and cold, beer, wine, water, iced tea, coffee, anything you could want to eat or drink.

There were two bed chambers, each with their own huge bathrooms with sauna, shower, hot tub, tanning booth, and a walk-in closet full of clothes.

Carl and Derek were astounded. Ther-Leh said, or thought, "We tried to make these rooms as comfortable as possible for you. If you need anything, put your hand on this pad, and I will come to see if I can help you." Ther-Leh pointed to a small green pad on the table.

"Ther-Leh," said Derek, "we have a lot of questions. Like…"

Ther-Leh cut him off, "Please, relax, cleanse yourselves, get comfortable. I'll be back in a little while. At that time I will answer your questions, and we will begin your training. Goodbye, for now." He turned, and vanished through the wall.

Chapter 9

Carl and Derek looked at each other. Carl
spoke first, "I need to get changed and get a
shower." Derek agreed. They decided they both
might as well get cleaned up and changed.
They didn't know if this was all a hallucination, or
what exactly, but the showers felt great and the
clothes in the closets were perfectly sized and
styled to suit their tastes.

After cleaning up and changing, they sat down
at the table and started to talk, and eat. Carl
grabbed a cold Guinness and put some fried
shrimp, three lobster tails, some scallops, and
hush puppies on a plate.

Derek got a latte and some turkey, stuffing,
mashed potatoes, gravy, cranberries, and a
cheeseburger.

Actually they were so hungry, and the food was
so good, neither of them said a word for at least
twenty-five minutes. Finally Carl said "You
know, for aliens, they sure can cook!" They both
laughed hysterically till tears were streaming
down their faces. It was like that was the
funniest thing they ever heard. After a couple of
minutes, the laughter subsided.

"Phew," said Derek, "I guess we needed that, after all we've been through today. Is your watch working?"

"No. I noticed it earlier, before I got in the shower. I wonder where we are, and how long we've been here." Carl pondered.

"Well, Ther-Leh said he would answer our questions when he came back, so I guess we'll find out soon enough. What do you think of all this? You know, the quarantine and these cards?" Derek had picked up one of the tokens they were given, and started looking at it a little closer.

"I don't know" said Carl, "they don't seem like they mean us any harm, but who knows for sure. I guess we have to trust them because I doubt if we can go too far. I would like to look around this ship some more though.

He walked to the point where they had entered the room, approximately, since there wasn't any door, he couldn't tell for sure, and tried to put his head through the wall to look around. Thunk. Solid wall. Hmmm. He stepped back a few paces, and walked toward the wall. Smap. Nose first into it. He moved a couple of feet to the left and tried again, without success.

71

"Well my boy-o, it looks like we're locked in." he exclaimed.

He sat back down and popped open another Guinness.

"Does that make us prisoners, do you think?" Derek asked.

"I guess. Although I really don't know where they think we're going to go. What say, time for some answers?" Carl said, with his hand over the green pad.

"Yeah." said Derek, "Call him."

Carl placed his hand on the pad. It glowed slightly until he removed his hand.

Then, almost instantly, there was Ther-Leh.

"Ahh," came the voice, "do you feel better?"

"Yes we do, thank you Ther-Leh." Carl said.

"How can I help you?"

"Can you answer our questions now? We have many."

"Yes, I'm sure you do. Go ahead and I will answer all that I can."

Derek asked the first question, "How are you communicating with us. Is it mental telepathy?"

"If you mean, am I using my mind to communicate with you, then yes, in a way. Actually, it's more like both of our minds, or, all three of our minds, are working together to hold conversations. This is the basic part of mind sway." This is something you will be taught as part of your training, before you leave."

"And when exactly will that be, and how long have we been here? And exactly where are we?" Carl asked.

"Well, you'll leave when you've completed your lessons. You've been here for two different amounts of time, that I will explain later, for now we'll say eleven Earth hours. And we are in orbit above our home, Plor-Jarj."

"What!?!" Derek screamed and jumped from the table. "Are you telling me, that in eleven hours, we've travelled a thousand light years?"

"Oh no, that only took eight minutes and fifty-two Earth seconds, we've been in orbit the rest of the time.

We are going to land, we just have to await the last data readings to be sure you don't pose a threat to our planet, even though you'll be in sealed containment suits."

Derek sat back down. He was struck dumb, even though he had tracked this ship a hundred times, and knew how fast it was, he couldn't grasp that he was this far from home, that fast.

But, we're going to be the first humans from Earth to see another world! Awesome, he thought.

"What powers this ship?" Derek asked

"A magnetic drive engine." Derek's eyes almost popped out of his head.

"Yes, the same type of engine you designed when you were seven years old, although yours was very primitive. That was one reason why you were picked for us to observe, you are a very smart human."

Then Carl spoke "That's one I've wondered about for a long time, how do you pick who to observe, and why ten years old?"

"We choose children with particular traits. At the age of ten, for Earthlings, or one-seventh of an average lifespan, all of the traits of adulthood are present, without any of the prejudices that are nurtured through the aging process. This is a common thread in most civilizations, at every evolutionary stage, everywhere.

That point is in all of them." Ther-Leh explained. "We call it 'reaching prime development'."

"I understand why then, you pick people like Derek here, he's very smart. But why did you pick me? I'm no genius, and never was."

"You had the traits of a great leader. And you exhibited a lot of perception. Not everyone can be a genius. And shouldn't be."

"What about all the other people on Earth that have these chips. We know of two-thousand and sixty-eight of them. Are there more? And what are their roles going to be in all of this?" asked Derek

"Yes, there are more. When you call them all together, you'll find that you have five-thousand. You, and they, will form Earth's 'Counsel for Universal Peace'. Your counsel will actually be the tutors, who will teach Earth how to live peacefully in the Universe. This is a required aspect of the training. We will teach you how to achieve all of this while you're here with us."

"Okay. Another question. Just to satisfy my scientific mind, how fast will this ship go, and how do you keep from running into things?" This was a big one for Derek, it's the one thing he'd wondered about since discovering the ship.

"As fast as we need it to, but not in the sense you think of as going fast.

When we went through the walls, we did so because the ship and everything in it was transparent.

That's why your sensors and tracking devices never picked us up coming towards Earth. We can travel at two, ten, or ten-thousand times the speed of light. If you haven't figured it out yet, we travel through time. That is the big secret to universal travel. We don't hit things because when we get to an object, neither us, nor the object, are really there at all, not at that moment. We go right through obstacles, until we slow down to below the speed of light. That's when your trackers pick us up. You've always thought we got out of range of your sensors, we actually just went too fast for them to follow."

"Ahhh," said Derek "Now it makes sense. Wow, that's amazing. All of this is because of the magnetic drive?"

"Yes."

"But, can you go through time in both directions, past I understand. Can you go into the future too?"

"Yes, that's very easy. I'm surprised you haven't figured out that part yet. We simply reverse the polarity of the magnetic drive to change direction through time.

For instance, when Carl asked how long you had been on the ship, I said there were two amounts of time for that question.

One answer was eleven Earth hours, and that was true. But, on Earth itself, one-thousand and thirty-six years had gone by."

"What?! We've been gone from Earth for over a thousand years. Everyone we know is gone?! What the hell are we going to do when we get back then? I thought we were supposed to lead the peace movement! How are we going to do that if all of our people are gone. What about our lab ? What.......?" Carl was beside himself.

"You're not listening. We move freely in both directions through time.

We could take you back to Earth twenty million years from now, or, we could take you back to the second we picked you up, which is what we will do. If there had been other people with you at the time we picked you up, you would be gone and back in less than a blink of an eye. No one would even know you were gone."

"You can really do that?"

"Yes."

"But this time we'll remember everything?" asked Derek.

"Yes, because this time we want you to. Oh and, we did know about the camera in your fingernail. You were picked because of your advanced intelligence, even for Earth people. We let your camera run and we installed the recognition image of me, actually.

We used that as the memory trigger so you could find the others. I'm sorry, but that will have to be enough questions for now. I just got clearance to take you to the disembarking area, so we can get you into your containment suits. The data said you are free from any threats to us."

"Then why do we have to wear the suits?" Carl interrupted.

" There are three reasons, mostly for your protection; we don't have lungs and don't breathe, so our atmosphere of methane and sulphur doesn't affect us, we're also impervious to the constant 423 degree surface temperature of our planet, and lastly, there is no water on our planet, therefore, no humidity. You would suffocate, your blood would boil, and you would dehydrate instantly as you left our ship. That is why you must wear the suits. It took me more than three hundred years to design them. I tried to balance functionality with efficiency and light weight. We should be going. Please follow me."

Ther-Leh headed towards and through the wall as Carl yelled for him to wait.

"Yes?"

"We can't go through the wall. I tried a little while ago, and I couldn't go through."

"That's because we locked the room, for your protection. We modify the atmosphere of wherever you are on the ship, to accommodate you. Otherwise, the temperature and atmosphere are what we're used to. You would die instantly if you had gotten out into the corridor without it being prepared for you. I assure you, you'll be able to go through now. Come along"

They again hesitated when they got to the wall, and glided right through. They went down the corridor for a good ways, still amazed at all the activity.

"Ther-Leh, how many Gilfeng are on this ship?" Carl asked.

"In Earth numbers, 340,000 or so."

Ther-Leh suddenly made a right turn and walked through the wall. Derek and Carl followed him and saw they were in a white room. In the middle of the room were two stands, each holding what looked like the full skin of a person.

79

"What the hell is this, who have you skinned?" wailed Carl.

"We haven't skinned anyone, these are your suits. They will protect you from everything in our atmosphere that can harm you, but you'll look exactly like you do without them.

We don't wear clothes, as you can see, so whether you want to put your clothes on over the suits, is entirely up to you, although I did design them to work without covering. You must undress now though, so I can help you get them on."

Both men undressed, for a moment Carl thought, I might like this place after all.

Then he realized what he was thinking and got to the task at hand. The men looked at the suits warily. Carl went to remove his from the stand but Ther-Leh stopped him.

"Everything should be adjusted for you to enter directly into the suits. Just stand in front of them, with your back to the suits, and step back. The suits will accept you and form to you automatically. I'm here to help in the case that I made any miscalculations."

"I don't know about this" said Derek. "It still looks like somebody's skin."

"I'll go first," said Carl, "then you go if I'm okay, alright?"

Derek nodded yes.

Carl turned around and back into his suit. How weird, he felt the suit accept him. It was like it had a secret zipper that opened and closed around him, but he didn't hear or feel anything. When he was in, he didn't feel anything at all. It was like he was still naked. Ther-Leh motioned for him to step forward, away from the rack. Carl took two steps forward. It really felt like there was no suit at all.

"How does it feel?" asked Ther-Leh.

"I can't feel it at all. It's great. This is really going to protect me from all the stuff you said is out there.?"

"I think so. We'll find out in a couple of minutes. Derek are you ready?" Ther-Leh asked.

Derek shrugged and backed into his suit. It was the strangest sensation he had ever felt.

He stepped away from his rack, and Ther-Leh asked him how his felt. All he said was, okay.

"Now," said Ther-Leh, "we will test it. I am going to start normalizing the atmosphere in this room. I will go gradually, until it matches the atmosphere outside. If you feel any discomfort, tell me immediately. Are you both ready?"

"As ready as ever, I guess!" said Carl.

These beings were amazing. Ther-Leh never moved a muscle, yet the entire feel of the room began to change.

They could tell the temperature was rising, they could feel a little dryness in their throats, and got the faintest smell and taste of sulphur. In a few seconds though, everything felt normal again.

"Why did you stop?" asked Carl.

"I didn't. The suit is just making it's own adjustments for your comfort. The room is still changing, keep alert to any problems."

After a few more minutes, Ther-Leh asked how they felt. They both said they felt fine.

Ther-Leh told them that the atmosphere was now fully changed over, the ship had landed, and they were ready to venture out to see Plor-Jarj.

"Are you ready?" he asked them.

"No time like the present." said Carl, "Whatcha say buddy?" he said, giving Derek a poke in the ribs.

"Whatever." said Derek. He did not look thrilled.

Ther-Leh picked up on this feeling, and was getting the monitoring data on Derek that told him that Derek was very nervous.

"Derek, it's alright to be nervous, you are about to do something no one else from your planet has ever done. You're going to step out into an inhabited world besides your own. But it will be okay. And so will you. I won't let anything happen to you, and I will always be near you.

You two are my charges, and I must protect you at all times." Ther-Leh, against Derek's normal train of thought, had actually given him some confidence.

"Okay, let's check it out!" he said.

Ther-Leh said, "Get ready, we are going down through the floor, so don't be alarmed."

Chapter 10

In a second, Carl and Derek were on the surface. You couldn't say "on the ground", because there wasn't any.

They were standing on something, but they couldn't tell what. The surface was the same glowing gold that the Gilfeng were. It was a little spongy, but supported them perfectly. Both men, at first, thought balance felt like it could be a problem, but it wasn't. Then they looked up and saw the city.

Both of their jaws dropped.

The city looked like it was made up of a million of the Gilfeng, but it was huge. It was hard to guess how big it was, or how far or close it was. It looked as if it was many miles tall.

Then Carl turned around to look at the ship, and again was in awe. The ship went out of sight, in all directions. It actually seemed to blend right into the planet.

Ther-Leh broke into their awe.

"Well, what do you think of Plor-Jarj?" he asked.

"Is that a city, or just big Gilfeng?" asked Derek.

"That is our capital city, Melij-Beneb. I guess you've noticed that Plor-Jarj, Melij-Beneb, and our ship all appear to be much the same as the Gilfeng. That's because we come from the planet, and we are all part of it, and it's part of all of us." explained Ther-Leh.

He could tell that they weren't getting it. "We aren't *from* Plor-Jarj, we are *of* Plor-Jarj. You haven't evolved far enough to understand this fully yet, but you will. It will also happen on Earth. Aren't the people of Earth, and the Earth, basically made up of the same compounds? You and your world are all carbon-based. You already are much the same, you just have to evolve more. Come, let's go to the city. We will get you settled in, and begin your training."

They set off across the expanse towards the city. Carl noticed that Ther-Leh had melded into the planet and was attached. He was moving across the surface like a boat on a pond, except there was no wake.

"When does it get light?" Derek asked.

Ther-Leh stopped, but didn't answer right away. Finally he asked, "What do you mean?"

"Well it's dark now. What time is morning? When does your sun rise? You know, how long is your day?"

85

"Ahh, I see what you're asking now. Sorry. We don't have a sunrise. We've made our atmosphere black, to keep out the light from our star. You see, it's so big, and so hot, that in our thin atmosphere, our planet would dry up and shrivel very quickly. Our makeup is selenium, silicon, and gold. Traces of phosphorous give us our inner glow. One day, in about six million years, you'll have to do the same thing on Earth, as your sun begins to grow."

Derek continued, "So if you don't have a night or day, how do you keep track of time?"

"We don't. There's no use for time. We all do what we do. All of the Gilfeng have jobs to do. We do them when it's time to, and we enjoy our time off as any other civilization does."

"What's your job, Ther-Leh?"

"I would have thought that was obvious, I'm a Universal Code teacher. I teach the Code, and how to convey it, to beings from other worlds. It's a very important job. Otherwise the universe would be full of all kinds of beings starting wars and taking over planets. Our purpose in the universe is to assure the peace. You could say that Plor-Jarj is the peace police of the universe."

"How long have you been doing this?" Derek asked.

"Hmm, almost twenty-three.....no, twenty-four thousand years. Earth years, that is."

"How old are you?!" asked Carl.

"Twenty-four thousand Earth years."

"You started working when you were a baby?" asked a surprised Carl.

"Baby?" Ther-Leh wondered, "Ah yes, you still give birth and grow to adulthood. We don't have babies here. When we come to be, we are ready to take our position in society. This will be covered in more detail in your lessons. First, I will teach you how to unlock the unused portions of your minds, which are very large. You will be amazed when you find out what your minds are capable of. Then, you'll learn the history of Plor-Jarj, then neighboring civilizations, eventually we'll make it to your part of the universe, and beyond. Next you will learn of the vast variety of life forms in the universe. And last, I will teach you the Universal Code. After all of this, you'll be tested, to be sure you have learned your lessons. When you have passed your tests, I will validate the cards I gave you, and I will instruct you how to convince your world that you are members of the Universe.

Then, we'll take you back to Earth and deposit you back in your laboratory, at the second we took you.

Once back on Earth, then your work will begin, as you teach your planet how to become a member of the Universe."

"Wow," said Derek to Carl, "It sounds like we're going to learn an awful lot of stuff. Ther-Leh, how long do you think this training will take."

"If the mind training goes well, your memory will become ten-thousand times more powerful than it is now. You should be able to remember everything I teach you very quickly. So I would say three to ten Earth years."

"Three to ten, sounds like a sentence! Things are still going to change on Earth, like the people we know." Carl blubbed.

"Oh no Carl, but your wrong about how long you've been gone. You see, on Earth, nobody will ever know you've been gone. As I said before it will only be a split second. But, here, time is different, you've been with us for thirteen hours, but on Earth, you've already been gone almost fifteen-hundred years."

"What?!? You mean us and everyone we ever knew have been dead for over fifteen-hundred years? What the fuck! Or, umm, wait, so, I don't know. I can't figure this out at all."

Now Carl was officially freaked out.

"Carl! This is why we don't need time. It's irrelevant.

When we take you back to Earth, nothing will have changed, not you, not the rest of the people, or the planet. It will be exactly as you left it. What will change, is what comes afterwards. You, and Derek, are going to be the people that will change your world, for the better. Trust me, as your lessons progress, it will all become clear to you. But now, we are here at the city. I've set up an apartment for you. I've placed this plaque on the wall, so you'll know where your quarters are later."

There was a plaque, about a foot square, on, or in, the wall. It was a little hard to tell. It was certainly easy enough for them to recognize. It had a picture of the Earth on it, and "Earth" in a beautiful gold script below it.

"Let's get you settled." said Ther-Leh.

They entered this building the same way they've entered everything since this whole ordeal started, through the wall.

It may have been getting a little easier, but not much.

They found themselves in a suite, almost exactly like the one they were in on the ship. When they entered, Carl and Derek both felt it get cold for a second, and they thought they smelled fresh air. Then it was gone.

Ther-Leh turned to them. "This is your suite where you will live for the time you're here. If there is anything you would like changed, please let me know.

There are some things I need to tell you about being here. This room is set for your atmosphere. You can keep the suits on while you're here, but you don't need to. To get out of the suit, you back into the rack, and the suit will let you out. I have installed a fail-safe system that won't let you leave the room unless you have your suit on. As we discussed before, that would be fatal. If you would like to look around, put on the suit, and you can go wherever you like. I will leave you a map after I've taught you some of the basics of living on Plor-Jarj. There is a standard model food dispenser over here at the table. I have loaded all of the Earth foods I could, about four-hundred thousand combinations. All you have to do is direct a thought of what you would like at the dispenser, and it will be served on the table for you. As Earthlings, I know you need rest and food.

I try to make sure everything is satisfactory on both scores. Here is a paging pad. It works the same as the one on the ship. I will always be close. I'm going to leave you for a while now. Eat, relax, sleep, whatever you like. Remember, there are no clocks here, and we will perform your training at your schedule. I will check on you later, and call me if you need anything. Goodbye for now."

Ther-Leh turned and was gone through the wall.

Carl and Derek sat down at the table and looked at each other.

Carl broke the silence. "I could use a rum and coke." he said. He looked at the box at the end of the table, and thought, "Rum and Coke."

They heard a small quick hum, and silently a rum and coke appeared.

Carl picked it up and took a sip. He said, "Tastes like home."

Derek looked at the box and thought, "Iron City beer."

Quick hum and, Iron City, ice cold.

"No kiddin'." he said.

"Ya gotta admit buddy," Carl said, "he sure does know how to accommodate. Cheers!"

They toasted and slurped their drinks, and fell quiet again for a long while.

Chapter 11

Derek broke the silence this time. "Is this all for real? Is it a dream? I know I was tired as hell from watching the ship all night, am I just sleeping."

"I don't think so bro'. If you are, than I am too, and we're having the same dream."

"I was afraid of that."

"Why?" Carl questioned, "Look, it appears that the Gilfeng are all about peace. They're going to teach us how to convince Earth to be a peaceful planet, so that we can get along with the rest of the universe. This is all good. Isn't this what we've been working for, for all these years?"

"Yeah, but...."

"But what? I thought you'd be giddy with excitement over all this."

"Me too. It's just that something doesn't seem right. I can't put my finger on it, but something's just off. Like, Ther-Leh said we're going to be the ones to teach the human race how to live within the universe.

93

Okay, that sounds nice, but he also said that it took the Gilfeng seven-thousand years to break their quarantine?

Maybe the Gilfeng live twenty-thousand years, but we don't. And his time calculations, how could we have been gone from Earth for over fifeen-hundred years, in what, twenty hours now. It doesn't make any sense."

"I don't know either" said Carl, "but I hope this is real. It gives hope for the future of the Earth, and mankind. And if it is for real, a lot of it doesn't make sense, but maybe that just shows how little we do know, as humans. I mean, here are living beings that are made of stuff we would never dream could be alive, in a place we would never think to look for life of any kind. Yet, here they are. And apparently, there are a whole hell of a lot more out there, that could be even stranger. I don't know about the time thing, or how we're supposed to do all the things Ther-Leh said we're supposed to do, but I'm willing to listen."

"Whatever, I guess all we can do is wait and see what happens. Should we eat?" Derek said a little more lightly.

"Why not. Let's see." Carl looked at the food dispenser and said, "Lobster tail, a nice rare filet mignon, corn on the cob, mashed potatoes, and a cold Guinness, please."

Nothing.

"Hey what gives, is this thing broke already?"

Derek piped up, "He said we had to think what we want, remember?"

"Oh yeah, that's right"

Carl looked at the box and thought his menu. A quick hum, and there was the prettiest dinner you could want.

He laughed, "This is friggin' great man!"

Derek laughed and thought up a dinner. They ate and talked some more about the happenings of the last fifteen hours or so. Derek was settling down and starting to get into the fact that this was a wonderful first-hand experience he had dreamed about a million times through the years. They each had a few beers while they talked and were getting a little tipsy and tired.

They looked around the suite and decided they might as well get some rest.

"Do you want to wear the suit, or take it off?" Derek asked Carl.

"I think I want to take it off and get a quick shower before I go to sleep." he answered.

"Okay. I guess I will too then."

The racks for the suits were in the bedrooms. Carl backed into his rack and the suit left him like it was drawn to a magnet. He realized that he could feel the air a little better in his lungs, and he could definitely feel the coolness of the air. It was refreshing in itself. Not that the suit was oppressive, maybe just a little restrictive. He took his shower, and went back out to the table. He thought up another beer, and was about halfway through it when Derek came out from the shower.

"How ya feel now buddy?" Carl asked him.

"Okay. The suit still creeps me out. Other than that, the shower felt nice."

"Well, I think I'm gonna finish this, and hit the hay."

"Allright, I'm gonna go ahead in. I'll see you in the morning, er, well, I'll see you when we wake up. Whenever that will be. Another ten-thousand years I guess." Derek laughed with his last line. "Later." he said, and was off.

Carl did finish his beer, then went in to lay down. He laid in the king bed and wondered if the glow of the room would keep him awake. That lasted for about ten seconds, and he was asleep.

Derek woke up first. He went to the bathroom, then went out to go to the table. Good thing he went to the bathroom, because he walked out to the main room and there was Ther-Leh. It scared him to death. Ther-Leh saw his reaction and apologized profusely, explaining that he didn't mean to shock him, he just thought he should be there when they awoke. Derek said it was okay, once he got over the shock. Carl heard Derek talking and got up too.

"Morning Ther-Leh! How are you today, my silicone and selenium friend?" Carl asked almost jovially.

"I'm well Carl, thank you for asking. I'm afraid I gave Derek a bit of a surprise though, being here when he awoke."

"So what's today's plan?" Carl wondered.

"I will take you on a tour of Melij-Beneb. I'll show you every place you may go in the city. Teach you the basic mannerisms you will need to interact with the Gilfeng. And begin your mind training. That's very important because everything else you learn, will be controlled by the capabilities of your minds."

"Ther-Leh," Derek broke in, "you said we would be the ones to teach our world the Universal Code.

But it sounds like something that could take a long time. I mean, we're humans, and therefore limited by our relatively short lifespan. How are we supposed to do this task when we get home?"

"Oh that's already been taken care of. The cards I gave you have altered your physiology, you will live forty to fifty thousand Earth years."

Neither Derek nor Carl knew what to say to that.

"The one thing that is common to all life forms, is adaptability." Ther-Leh continued. "It is what makes populating the universe possible. Most civilizations figure that out rather quickly. You will adapt, like all of the rest, in your own way of course, and to your particular surroundings."

"But living forty or fifty thousand years isn't adapting, it's changing the rules of life, as we know it." said Carl.

"Life, as you know it, is already changed. Let's start your learning process. That may help you to understand a lot of what's to come. The biggest obstacle to understanding is your own mind. Minds, and civilizations, grow according to what they're taught. They're taught what society is accustomed to. Thus, anything that doesn't conform to pre-conceived ideas, makes no sense.

I know you've seen this on your planet. Every time a scientist discovers something, or an inventor has an idea, that disputes an accepted theory, other members of the community say it's nonsense. This is where your minds are right now. I'm going to teach you to open your minds to any and all perceptions of any situation. But first, you must release all thoughts of how things should be, and accept that anything truly is possible. It's actually easier than it sounds. You don't have to forget anything, or alter your way of thinking, you just need to unlock the part of your mind you don't use. With your race, it's a large part. We know that most Earthlings use only about six percent of their available mind power. You, Derek, are considered a genius on Earth, yet you use only about eight percent of your mind. I am going to help you unlock the rest of your brain. When that happens, you will find it much easier to believe that anything is possible."

"How exactly do you do this mind expansion?" Derek wanted to know.

"First, I'll teach you to look out, with your mind. The best way to do that will be to let you look at my mind. Then, I'll teach you to look into your own mind. When you learn how to do that, you will see all the parts of your mind you have never used.

Then, you'll be able to employ them, to form a more complete picture of the universe around you." said Ther-Leh.

"Will you teach us both at the same time, or individually?" asked Carl.

"Individually. It's easier than trying to coordinate two minds. I'll start with you Carl."

"Why me? Derek is a genius, he should be able to do this much easier."

"Actually, because his mind is a little more developed, he will find it somewhat harder to wander from his strictly ordered way of thinking. Before we start though, I would still like to take you on a tour of the city. There are some things you need to see, as they concern you alone. Get into your suits, and we'll go."

The men went into their rooms and entered their suits. There were a few seconds of acclimation, then the suits felt like their skin. They went back out, and left through the wall with Ther-Leh. It was getting a little easier each time.

There were throngs of Gilfeng everywhere. They were moving in all directions.

"Where are they all going?" Derek asked Ther-Leh.

"They're going about their business. Doing what they do. As I said before, everyone has a job on Plor-Jarj."

"But, what are their jobs? You said you don't eat or sleep. I mean, what is there for them to do?"

"Remember I also said we were the peace police of the universe? That is what most of us do. There are about seventeen million of us. Approximately twelve million of us spend all of our time working with other worlds, in many ways. The rest of the population takes care of running Plor-Jarj. I'll explain more of this later, right now we are where we need to be. Come." Ther-Leh turned to the left and walked through a wall next to another plaque with the Earth on it.

When Carl and Derek entered the room, they were in awe. It appeared to be a library. But what a library. It was round, about thirty feet in diameter, but went up.......and up.........and up. They literally couldn't see to the top, it just faded into nothing. There was what looked like a small, clear, elevator car on two thin poles, next to the wall. The poles also went up to......infinity maybe? Probably not, but close. In the center of the room was a round counter with a chair on each side, and two computers maybe, on the counter.

Ther-Leh projected, "This is your resource center.

I have made this to be somewhat like a library on Earth, but of course there is a lot more information here. To find a book, you will enter your question on the computer, it will locate that volume, and tell the travel pod where to go. You will board the pod and it will take you to the desired location. These aren't actually books, they are disc folders that will play on the computers."

"What kind of stuff is on the discs?" asked Carl.

"Each disc set contains all the information available, from every civilization in the universe."

"How many are there, Ther-Leh?" Derek asked.

"At this time, we know of almost three million inhabited worlds in the universe. And we have only explored twenty-eight percent of the known universe."

"What?!? How come the scientists on Earth haven't been able to find any signs of life?" Carl yelled.

"Because they simply don't know how to look. Yet. They look for conditions that could support life as they know it. They're looking for other. humans. That, they'll never find, because they are unique, as are all life forms. That's the key, you must be able to recognize life, in all of its forms.

Strangely enough, Earth has more life forms on it, than most planets. Most have one, maybe two types of beings. Yet, on Earth, there are thousands of species, that live in all kinds of conditions. But the scientists still look for the perfect human habitat."

"This is what you're going to teach us, how to look properly?" Derek asked.

"Yes, among other things. Actually most of that, you will teach yourselves, in this room. Once you've learned to master the power of your mind, you'll be amazed at how quickly you will be able to learn. That's enough here for now, we have other places to see. I would like for all of your areas to be in one location, but it's impossible. That's why I'm taking you around, and will provide you a map. Also, I suppose you've noticed the plaques. Any place where there is a plaque with the Earth on it, is an area designed just for you two and no one else. That is how you're to identify your learning and recreation areas.

You will no doubt notice all of the other plaques, there are plaques for every species of being that is here being trained. I have one hundred and forty-two students, at the moment. Two from each of seventy-one worlds."

"Are all of our areas on the ground floor?" Carl wondered.

"Yes, because you can't levitate, and unfortunately never will be able to. Also, the upper levels are reserved for support teams and research.But, and this is very important, don't attempt to enter any other world's area. The suits should prevent you from doing so, but we have found in the past, that it is possible. If you were to enter another world's realm, it would probably kill you."

They came to another wall with an Earth plaque on it. They entered into a gym/spa/track room. It was very nice. There was all kinds of exercise equipment, a track around the wall, about twelve feet off the floor, a pool with a small waterfall, showers, and a sauna. One end of the room opened out into an entertainment area. In the middle of the room, there was a poker table, of all things, a credenza with all kinds of games, cards, dice, and paper and pencils for scoring. On one side was a giant screen tv, a stereo system, a couple of overstuffed chairs and a food dispenser. On the other side of the room was a bed, and a large steel cylinder against the wall.

"I know you will want to stay fit while here, and I know you will want to relax at times. I've tried to think of everything you might need or want, but again let me know if there is anything I can do to make your time here more comfortable. The television and stereo menus are on the screen, and are thought controlled."

"What's with the bed and the tube on the wall?" Carl asked.

"That's another invention I came up with for you. There are pictures of one-thousand Earth women in the memory of that machine, you only need to push a button to choose one, and she will be cloned and available for your sexual satisfaction. When you're finished, the woman will return to the chamber for recycling. I know this is very important for earth men." Ther-Leh sounded very proud of what he had built for his wards.

"You really have thought of everything for us Ther-Leh. I gotta hand it to ya buddy!" Carl said. "What do ya think, bro?" He punched Derek's arm.

" Yeah, he thought of everything. Thanks Ther-Leh." Derek didn't seem very impressed.

"You'll have to excuse Derek," Carl loudly whispered to Ther-Leh, "scientists are always such bores. HAHA!!"

Carl was having a wonderful time on his first day on Plor-Jarj. Derek was not.

Chapter 12

"The more he shows us, the more he tells us, the less I like it!" screamed Derek.

"Dude, why are you freaking out? What the hell is there that's not to like?"

Carl was trying to understand Derek's reactions to all of this, but couldn't quite grasp his apprehension.

"Carl, don't you think it's just a little *too* perfect? Don't you think it odd, that this creature knows every little thing we think about? Everything we could possibly want? I mean, what's really his plan for us?"

"No, I don't," said Carl, "they've been watching our development for twenty-thousand years. These chips have been in our arms since we were ten. This guy has been doing this forever. I'd say he's just mastered his job, and does it very well. Why can't you just relax and try to enjoy all of this?"

"Because I'm a scientist and I question everything. And I still just don't feel right. I really am sorry to be such a drag, but I can't shake this feeling." Derek said apologetically.

Ther-Leh had given them a map of this section of the city, and some instructions for interacting with other Gilfeng. Avoid collisions with Gilfeng, you will pass through them, and they don't particularly like that. Don't try to initiate communication with them. They know why you're here, and who you are. Some Gilfeng may talk to them though. Mostly it will be other members of Ther-Leh's team. Don't try to enter other world's areas, or unauthorized Gilfeng areas, it could be fatal. Other than that, they could go and do what they pleased. Ther-Leh said he would be back later to continue their lessons.

"Are you hungry?" Carl asked.

"Not really."said Derek.

"You wanna go to the gym, or rec hall?"

"No. I think I may lay down for a while. You go ahead if you want though."

"Yeah, I think I will. I'll be back in a while."

"Okay. Carl?"

"Yeah?"

"Be careful, okay? I don't want to wind up in this circus alone, alright?"

"Okay, I'll watch my back." Carl said as he went through the wall.

Carl was glad he had the map, everything looked the same, except for plaques here and there. He looked at some of them. The writing was interesting, and there were so many different looking worlds.

He found the workout room and entered noiselessly. Ther-Leh said they didn't need to wear the suits when they were in their own areas, so Carl backed up to his rack and stepped out. It was quite a trip because every time he could feel the change for a minute and was a pretty good rush. He was a little hungry, so he sat at the table and tried to figure out what he wanted to eat. What the hell he thought, how about a small lobster tail, drawn butter, and some steak fries. Hummmm, click, out came his food. Oh, and a Guinness he thought. Hummmm, click, one cold Guinness. He sat and ate his food and drank his beer. He stopped to check out the sound system. Let's see, Ther-Leh said this is thought controlled. Um, music menu, he thought. The screen lit up a soft blue. A menu for albums and singles, listed alphabetically came up on the screen.

Hmmm, he thought, Bob Seger, Against the Wind. The music started, very quietly. Carl thought, louder, and the music started getting louder, slowly. When it got to a nice level, Carl thought stop. The volume settled where it was. Very cool he thought.

He finished up his meal and looked at the cylinder against the far wall. He had to check this out. He walked across the room to the tube and noticed a ten by ten inch screen on the left side of the tube. He touched the screen and it lit up with a picture of a beautiful blond, naked, and hot. There were small marks in both of the lower corners of the screen and two marks in the center bottom. He touched the right one and the picture changed to another hot blond. He touched the left one and it went to the first girl. He touched the left again and it went to a smoldering brunette. He started pushing the left button and scrolled through about thirty pictures, when he got to a girl he recognized. It was the stewardess from the flight he had taken to Bonn. She was naked, of course, and was pretty sweet. He pushed the button again and the girl in the picture was one of the volunteers that worked in the lab from time to time. He always wondered what she looked like with no clothes on. Then he got an idea. He began pushing the right button rapidly until he got back to the blondes.

110

It was then that he realized who the first blond girl was, it was Gretchen. Good god he wished now he would have tried to hook up with her, she was exquisite. He looked at the two middle buttons. One looked like a circle with a line down the middle. The other looked like a circle that was cut in half and opened up. He pushed this one. The tube made a quiet hiss. Then the door opened.

Gretchen stepped out and leaned right against him. Her bare breasts pushed against his naked chest and he felt his manhood rising to the occasion. Gretchen said "How nice to see you again Mr. Haskins." She then laid a serious liplock on him and pushed him back on the bed. Carl was delirious with pleasure as this clone made love to him in ways he couldn't even fantasize about. It was incredible. Afterwards, they laid together for some time, cuddling. Carl finally got up and went to the tube, and pushed the close button. Gretchen got off the bed, walked to the tube, kissed Carl and said good bye, and stepped in. A quiet hiss, and the door closed. The screen asked "Would you like to save Gretchen as a favorite? Yes or no."

He pushed "Yes".

Carl thought, as he stood in the shower, Derek must be crazy, it can't get any better than this, at least I hope he is, cause I sure don't want this to end.

When Carl stepped through the wall to go out, he was almost run over by two blue and orange flames, about four feet tall. He thought he heard a voice of some sort, when they went by. He watched as they moved about twenty feet farther and then turned left and went through a wall.

"Wow" he said to himself, "They must have been living beings."

"Hello Carl." he heard in his head. He turned to find a Gilfeng standing in front of him, "I'm Vla-Hurd. I'm part of Ther-Leh's research team. Glad to meet you."

"Like wise" said Carl.

"What do you think of Plor-Jarj so far."

"So far, so good."

"Good. I have to go now, but I will see you again." Vla-Hurd said.

"Okay, nice to meet you." said Carl. But Vla-Hurd was already thirty or forty feet away, moving at a pretty good pace.

This place is so wild, Carl thought, as he walked back to the suite.

When he got there, Derek was gone. On the table, there was a note, spelled out in corn, that just said "Library". Carl laughed. I wonder how he decided on corn, he thought?

Carl decided he might as well go over and see what Derek was doing. He walked into the library and found Derek at the desk cussing and yelling for Ther-Leh.

"Where are you, you silicon freak? What the hell is this all about? Come on, do whatever it is you're going to do!!"

"Derek, what's wrong?"Carl asked, rushing across the room.

"Look! Look at the screen! It says 'The Earth was destroyed by its own warring civilization in their year 2015. Universal day 26.24561 to the 256th power.' Destroyed! Now do you understand?! They're going to destroy the Earth! I knew this wasn't right! Dammit!!"

"Derek! Settle down. Maybe that's why we're here. Maybe this is how they saw our future, and brought us here, to teach us how to go back and change history. If this stuff about time traveling is for real, you have to be able to use it to make changes." Carl suggested.

"So now you're an expert on time travel?" Derek sneered.

"No, but I'm also not freaking out over an entry in a book, without finding out some more information!" Carl snapped back. "What information?! Can you say, without a shadow of a doubt, that Ther-Leh hasn't told us anything that isn't just what he says? Are you one hundred percent sure that we can totally trust everything he says? Eh?" Derek prodded.

"Uhhh....yeah! I believe him. A hundred percent!"

"Bull" said Derek, "If you really believed that, you wouldn't have started your answer with 'Uhhh....'. You know as well as I do, that we really don't know, for sure, what their plans are for us."

"You may be right, my friend, but I don't think, at this point, that there's a lot we can do about it. We're a long way from home, both in time and space. So for the moment, we'll just have to go along with Ther-Leh's plan. But we'll keep our heads about us, and keep looking for signs that he's putting us on." Carl assured Derek.

"Okay, you're right that we can't do much about it, but yeah, let's not drop our guard just yet."

Chapter 13

It had been three months, although they didn't know it. The things they were learning were amazing. They were learning how to reach unused portions of their minds. Information was filling the empty spaces as soon as they were discovered. And, they were learning how to see other beings minds. Well, Ther-Leh and Vla-Hurd's anyway.

And, they were learning how much life there was out in the universe. They had already been introduced to about a fifth of the inhabited planets in this region of the universe. It amounted to about six-hundred. They had no idea there would be so many.

At this point in their training, they could absorb the entire history of a world, and its life forms, in about thirty to fifty minutes. They were learning at breakneck speed. They had stopped talking to each other because it really was easier to talk with their minds.

What they hadn't learned yet, was how to block someone from seeing parts of their minds they didn't want seen. It was starting to lead to some problems.

"What do you mean I'm too stupid to understand?" Carl thought towards Derek.

"You're not a scientist is all. I don't think you're really stupid. You just don't know how this stuff works." Derek thought back. He tried hard not to think his next thought, but he couldn't keep his mind from thinking it, "Asshole."

"Bite me!" thought Carl. He went into his room and got into his suit. He walked past Derek, and through the wall without a thought. "At least we can't read each other's minds from any distance." he thought.

He walked through Melij-Beneb, just wandering, until he found himself at the rec center. He went in and removed his suit. He put on some music and sat down on the couch. "How are we ever going to bring peace to Earth, if we can't even get along?" he asked out loud. His own voice startled him a little. He hadn't spoken out loud for quite some time, maybe five or six weeks, or three, or seven, who knew. In this crazy timeless world, he couldn't even guess how long a day was. Ten hours, thirty hours, again, who knew.

Timekeeping, or the lack of it, was the thing that seemed to be affecting Carl and Derek the most. It was hard for them to figure out when they should eat, sleep, exercise, read, anything.

116

When they did go to sleep, they would wake up, and wonder how long they had been sleeping.

But every day, Ther-Leh, Vla-Hurd, or other members of the training team would come to them and teach. There were a number of teachers, all with different subject specialities. Ther-Leh, of course, was the team leader. Vla-Hurd was number two, and answered all of Carl And Derek's general questions. Gij-Llemdr taught about the make up of different lifeforms. Ouj-Yigd taught planetary composition. Hyiv-Megdrl was the communication expert. And on and on. It seemed to Derek that there were about twenty Gilfeng on Ther-Leh's team. Knowledge of the Universe was flowing into their minds like water into the ocean.

They were tested constantly. Language test; "Alvrod geoude bunjmem tregdor ybunm." "Language, planet, and translation, please." Hyiv-Megdrl would say.

"Raudiscin, from Peonornifootch three. Are you a counsel member?" would be the answer.

Planetary composition; Planet: carbon, liquid nitrogen, mercury, cobalt, zvrytium, and chezgvern. Atmosphere, ammonia, pyolitigum, and shletsgilfim.

Eczvlotim, in the Argraxis system.

And so it went, day after day.

Carl decided to have a beer and a snack while he was listening to the music. He thought up an Oatmeal Stout and some nachos with cheese. After a couple of minutes, he got up and turned off the music and turned on the TV. He flipped through the channels for a minute and then turned it off. He really wished there were more humans around to talk to. He thought about the clones. "I guess it's better than nothing" he thought.

He went to the machine and flipped through the pictures. He stopped at a cute little brunette, and pushed the open button. She stepped out of the machine and pushed herself up against him. She was awfully cute, but he didn't want sex right now. He backed up a couple of steps and asked her what her name was.

"I'm Marjorie." she said. And she moved up against him again.

He gently pushed her away and said "I don't want to have sex right now, I just want to talk."

She got a puzzled look on her face, "Talk?"

"Yes." said Carl, "I just want to talk. Where are you from? Do you have family? What do you do for a living?

Anything you would like to talk about really. I just need someone besides Derek to talk to."

"I....I....I don't know any of the things you're asking. I am here to satisfy your sexual desires, that's all." She was very confused about what Carl was asking her.

"Okay, let's go more slowly. One question at a time. Where are you from?"

"The machine." she said. She moved up against Carl again.

This time he pushed her harder than he meant to, and she fell. As she fell, she hit her head on the corner of the table. She got back up and turned to Carl. His jaw dropped.

Carl was stunned. Marjorie had a large cut on the right side of her scalp. It was so big that the skin had formed a flap and was hanging down. Under it Carl saw bright shiny metal.

"I thought you were a clone!" Carl screamed.

"No, I'm a robot. I was built by Ther-Leh to provide you with sex."

"What?! But the pictures. Ther-Leh said you were a cloning program, and real. Kind of."

"No" she said "I'm a changling robot. I can take on whatever form my controller desires."

He had been screwing a robot all this time.

Carl turned and pushed the close button. She quietly entered the cylinder, and it closed with a click and a hum.

This was the first time he had caught Ther-Leh in a lie.

Chapter 14

Carl donned his suit and hurried back to their suite.

"Derek, are you here?" he called aloud.

"Yeah. Look, I'm sorry about the thought earlier-"

Carl cut him off, "That's okay, listen, I have been pretty blindly following along with everything, up to this point. But, I'm going to slow down now. I just found out something Ther-Leh wasn't exactly truthful about."

"What?" asked Derek.

"The girls in the tube, in the rec room? They're not clones, they're not even a they, it's a robot. We've been screwing a robot for crissakes!"

"Not 'We' buddy, you. I haven't touched that thing. I didn't like the idea from the start, whatever was in there. So how have you liked screwing a robot, anyway?"

Carl wasn't finding any humor in this.

"Fine, until I found out what she is, if it even is a she." Carl said, visibly shaken.

121

"Well, I'd say if she's a robot, she's more like an 'It'."

This didn't help Carl at all.

"Of course" Derek continued, "this only makes me wonder even more, what else has Ther-Leh told us that isn't exactly true?"

"I didn't want to tell you about some of the oddities I've found because I didn't want to freak you out, or me for that matter. But early on, when I was in the library, I looked for the info on Plor-Jarj. There's nothing about it, or the Gilfeng. I thought that was strange. So I really started to pay attention. Like I went out and just hung out in front of our suite for a while. Well, for a city of 12 million, I only saw two Gilfeng the whole time. I was out there for an hour or so."

"How do you know how long you were out there?" Carl broke in.

"I counted it out, second by second. The thing is, there is something off here. I just wish I knew what's going on."

"Well, I want some answers, I'm going to call Ther-Leh!"

Carl headed for the call pad but Derek stopped him.

"Wait" he said, "I'm not sure just coming out and asking Ther-Leh what the hell is going on, is the right thing to do.

We may not like the answer we get. Let's give it a little more time, and let me do a little more research. There are a couple of things I want to try."

"Like what?" Carl asked.

At that moment, things went from possibly bad, to definitely worse. Ther-Leh entered the room through the wall and went straight to Carl.

"You've commited one of the worst crimes you could. You'll have to be quarantined" Ther-Leh thought.

Immediately Carl felt like he was caught in a vise. His arms sucked into his sides, and he couldn't breathe. At all! Ther-Leh headed out and Carl followed him, totally against his will. It was like Ther-Leh had hog tied him, and was dragging him along.

Derek protested "Wait a minute Ther-Leh, where are you taking him? I demand to know!"

Ther-Leh never even slowed down. And out they went.

Carl passed out from lack of oxygen as soon as they left the room.

When he came to, he couldn't figure out at all where he was, or what he was in. He couldn't move any part of his body. He felt like he was encased in amber.

Like the prehistoric wasp he had at home. He also felt like there was a needle in his left arm. He became very scared at that moment.

Suddenly he heard Ther-Leh's thoughts.

"You made a very grave mistake Carl. You commited a violent act on Plor-Jarj. This is unacceptable. You will stay here until I think you have gotten over your violent thoughts. You will be provided with nutrition to keep you alive, but that is all."

"But you lied to us! What are you really doing with us?!? Come back here!   I want to know what the hell is happening!" Carl yelled with his thoughts. But Ther-Leh was gone. He was alone. He also just realized…….it was dark! And not just dark like night, no this was dark like being buried alive dark. Or the deepest cave with no flashlight dark.

He tried to move. His arms, his legs, his head, anything. But it was no use, whatever he was in was solid and wouldn't budge. He felt a tear come to his eye. Now, he was really scared.

124

Chapter 15

Derek pushed the call pad again and again. But
no Ther-Leh. He went in and put on his suit. He
thought he had to try to find Carl. But where
would he look? He had no idea where Ther-Leh
would have taken him. He just wondered what it
was all about. What violence did Carl commit?

He headed for the wall to leave, just as Ther-Leh
came in.

"What have you done with Carl? What's going
on? What did he supposedly do? Is he going to
get a trial?"

"Please Derek, calm down. Carl has issues with
violence. He tried to murder one of the cloned
females at the recreation center. We police the
universe, stopping violence, we also must stop it
here, on Plor-Jarj. Carl will be held in
suspension until he can release himself from
these feelings. It must be this way."

"He didn't try to murder a girl, he tried to tell a
sex robot he wasn't interested!"

"It's not who or what he tried to hurt, it's the
feelings and actions that have gotten him into
trouble."

125

"Well where is he? Can I visit him?" Derek begged.

"I'm afraid not. Don't worry about him though, the experience won't hurt him in any way. He just needs to think."

"What about me? He's my best friend. Even though he drives me nuts at times." Derek exclaimed.

"My team and I will try to help you keep your mind busy, so that you don't miss him too much. And he will only be in the holding area for a short time." Ther-Leh told him.

"So, what is the holding area, exactly?"

"It's a small section of Plor-Jarj that contains no gold or phosphorous, so it's completely dark. It's very good for thinking introspectively."

"You said he won't be there long. How long?" Derek was genuinely concerned for Carl.

"There is no set length to his quarantine. It will actually be up to him. I'll be monitoring his thought patterns, and will be able to tell when his violent thoughts have left him. Then he'll be released, and returned here."

Derek told Ther-Leh that he understood, and hoped that Carl got better soon.

126

He then thanked Ther-Leh for keeping him posted on Carl.

Ther-Leh assured him that it wouldn't be that long and left.

After Ther-Leh left, Derek thought how well he had covered his thoughts while with him. He probably would have wound up with Carl, if Ther-Leh had picked up on the thought Derek had, of wanting to see him dead. And of wanting to do it himself!

He sat down and tried to think of how he could find Carl. Problem was he had no idea where to start looking for him. Then he thought of the map. He got the map and looked for a spot that might be dark and devoid of gold and phosphorus. But all it showed was a crude representation of this part of the city, with the locations of the Earth zones.

Well, maybe he could find it if he just went out and started looking around. After all, Ther-Leh hadn't been gone that long and the Gilfeng really didn't seem to move too fast.

He stepped through the wall and kind of surveyed the surroundings with a new urgency. He decided to go to the left and see where it would take him. He was taking long strides, about one a second, and was counting the whole time.

After thirty-eight minutes and forty seconds, he reached the edge of the city abruptly.

  The edge of the city ended on his left and went off into the distance, until it faded away.

In front of him, Plor-Jarj stretched off to infinity. A plain of softly glowing gold spread out before him. He squinted off into the distance, but couldn't see any dark spots.

Been gone too long anyway he thought to himself. He turned around and went back, counting all the way. He eventually got back to the apartment, and kept going. Might as well try this way. After forty- five minutes, he once again decided he had gone too far. Again he turned back. This time when he got to the apartment, he went in.

He was thirsty and had to pee. He took a whiz and thought out a glass of water. He looked at the map some more while he drank. Still nothing.

He went back outside and figured this time he would try going into the city. He was glad he had brought the map as there were no straight walkways on this place. There were turns galore, this way and that, and he was sure he would have been hopelessly lost without the map. He wasn't altogether sure that he wouldn't wind up lost, even with the map.

He had walked around, and made a hundred turns, when he came to the first solid object he had seen on Plor-Jarj.

It was a large black block. It was about fifteen feet tall and thirty to forty feet long by maybe a hundred feet wide.

He touched it and it felt like a hot rock.

He thought, "Carl! Carl! Can you hear me?"

He walked all the way around the block, projecting thoughts to Carl, with no reply. He was sure this was where Carl must be. He thought harder, with more concentration, "Carl, can you hear me? Carl, can you hear me?". Then, "Derek, where are you?"

"I'm outside this huge, black block of what looks like rock. Where are you, are you inside? Are you in a room? Can you see a door?"

"No, I'm not in a room. I'm suspended in ……..I don't know, maybe the rock. I just know it's completely dark, and I can't move at all. Derek, you've got to find a way to get me out of here!"

Carl was almost frantic. "I'm going to try, buddy." Derek assured his friend. Although he had no clue how he was going to accomplish the task, he had to try.

Derek started walking around the block again, this time looking very carefully at the walls for any chink that may be an entry point. He found nothing. He needed to get on top, maybe that was how he could get in.

It was too tall to jump, and the sides were slick as a whistle. He looked at the buildings all around him. He wondered, since the buildings, Plor-Jarj, and the Gilfeng were all made of the same stuff, could he perhaps walk up the side of one of them and jump across? It looked like the only thing to try.

He picked a building close to where he had talked to Carl, and put his foot into the side of it. His foot went about four inches into the building and he put his weight on it. It gave a little, but felt like it might hold him. He raised his arms and dug his fingers into the gold goo and tried to pull himself up. It didn't work. It was like trying to climb Jell-O. He tried half a dozen times with no success. He then tried to jump up. But the planet below just gave way when he pushed off. He was getting frustrated very quickly.

"What are you doing Derek?" , it was Ther-Leh.

"Um, I'm just checking out the neighborhood." lied Derek. He hoped he was concealing his thoughts, but it didn't work.

"I don't think that's true, Derek" said Ther-Leh, "I think your trying to get to Carl. I can tell it's something you both want, so here's your wish granted!"

In an instant, Derek was in complete darkness and totally immobile.

"I can't imagine why you and Carl are finding it so hard to stay here. I've tried to make it as comfortable and homey as I could, and still, both of you are so suspicious that I have some evil plan for you. I can assure you, I don't. I just want to teach you the required lessons, and return you to Earth to do your jobs."

"Sure, that's why you lock us up like criminals?" thought Derek.

"No. Your *locked up* because neither of you seem to desire to do what you're supposed to. Carl attacked a cyborg, and you're out here trying to find and free him. You must get these thoughts out of your systems so we can proceed with your training. I'm going to leave you now. You must accept that I don't have any evil plan, and commit yourself to your lessons. I will return later to check on you."

"Wait, Ther-Leh. I'm sorry. I realize now that you're right. Let me out. Let me out of here you......." Derek thought he should stop there. " Ther-Leh? Ther-Leh, are you still there?"

There was no response.

"Carl? Carl, can you hear me?" he thought.

Again, no answer.

Great, he thought, now I've made things worse than they were.

"Carl!?" he thought harder.

Still no answer.

He started to sob quietly, then thought that Carl was in this thing somewhere, and exerted all the thought strength he could, "Carl? Can you hear me?!"

"Yes, where are you?" he finally heard.

"I'm in the stone, or, whatever this thing is."

"What?!? How did you wind up in here?"

"Ther-Leh caught me outside, and I lied when he asked me what I was doing. I guess lying isn't approved of here, so he put me inside. I had to use a lot of thought to reach you. He must have put me in the other end from you."

"What is one end? How big do you think this thing is?" Carl projected.

"It looked like a hundred feet long and forty or fifty feet wide."

"What's it look like?"

"A big black rock. It's hot on the outside. Funny it's not in here. But anyway, real smooth with like a matte finish."

"What was it like coming in here, could you feel it? I don't know cause I was knocked out and woke up in here."

"I don't know. One minute I was out, next minute I was in. It was like he thought me in here. He probably did actually. I'm sure he'll teach us everything we'll know, but he won't teach us everything he knows!"

Carl and Derek's thoughts were quiet for a few minutes. Finally, Carl mentally asked Derek, "What did he say we have to do, to get out of this thing?"

"He said we have to get violent and suspicious thoughts out of our heads. He said that when we were ready, he would let us out to continue our lessons."

"Well," Carl thought, "He can tell when our thoughts are honest and true, and when we're trying to hide something. I guess the only thing we can do is to convince ourselves that everything is all right, here on Plor-Jarj."

"That's not going to be easy, with the activities of the last three hours." said Derek.

133

"No, but we have to try. If we can convince Ther-Leh that we have seen our inner thoughts, and realize how crazy they are, maybe we can get out of here today."

"I just don't know how I can do it. I'm so pissed right now. Let me calm down a little and I'll see if I can fool myself into believing it."

"Okay" said Carl, "We'll try in a while. You let me know when you're ready."

Chapter 16

"Carl?"

"Yes, Derek?"

"How long have we been in here, do you think?"

"I don't know. I know I've slept sixteen times, but I don't know for how long each time."

Suddenly, Derek was outside of the box, near a corner. Then he realized Carl was also out, about 40 feet down the side if the box.

The two men walked towards each other. When they met, they hugged and wondered what had happened. But, before either of them could even get a question out, Ther-Leh appeared.

"Hello my friends." thought Ther-Leh.

"Hi Ther-Leh." Carl said, "Thank you for freeing us."

"Oh no, you did that yourselves. I've been monitoring your thought processes, and was pleased to see how easily you were able to retrain your thoughts so fast."

"I don't know why we've been so suspicious," Carl said, "it's just been a lot to process. I'm sorry."

"This is part of your training. This is the type of suspicion you'll endure when you reach your home again. Even your peers that have known you for a long time, will wonder what your motives are.

When we bring beings here, they're civilizations are at the crossroads. They can travel in space with limited agility, but still don't realize that there is a universe teeming with life, past their own little corner of it. As I told you when you first arrived, we are here to assure that the universe remains peaceful.

When you return to your Earth, your biggest challenge will be to get your kind to accept all of the things you've been taught here."

"Will our people really accept us? I mean, will we really be able to convince them that we've been here, and we need to learn the Universal Code?", Derek asked.

"Yes, with the ID cards we gave you. The cards can do an amazing array of things, but we control them. We will be monitoring you and your progress, and will activate the cards to perform missions as needed."

136

"What kind of missions?" asked Carl.

"All kinds. Early on, they will give credence to your story of traveling here and meeting us. Some of your final lessons will be how to present the cards when you return to Earth.

But enough of all of this for now, you've been in confinement for thirty four Earth days, so you should head back to your apartment. You probably want to eat and talk to each other face to face. I'll be around later to check on you and get you back to your lessons. Go eat and rest, I'll see you later."

Ther-Leh turned and sped away. Carl and Derek headed back to their apartment without talking. Once inside, they both sat at the table in silence for a short while. Carl was the first to speak.

"You know, now that I think about it, I am hungry. Thirty four days without a real meal is long enough. Whaddya say Bud? You hungry?."

"Sure." said Derek.

Carl could see that his friend was miles away, maybe even light-years.

"What's on your mind Buddy?", he asked.

137

"Oh, nothing I guess. I don't want to think the wrong thing and get us in trouble again, and you never know if anyone is listening in on our thoughts. It's just......never mind."

"It's okay, I know what you mean. Let's eat something."

Derek piped up with, "And drink!"

They both laughed and thought up a couple of nice meals and a few brews. After a few more brews, and a couple of shots, they both felt much better, and more tired.

"I don't know about you, but I'm ready for a nice shower, and a nap where I can move around if I want." said Carl, "I'll see you later on."

"Yeah, I think you've got the right idea. I'll see ya later. Thanks, Carl, for everything."

"No problem pal."

The shower felt so great, Carl almost fell asleep standing in the water. When he was finished, he laid down on the bed, and was asleep before he knew it. And he dreamed.

He dreamed he was home again, on his mountain, on his porch, looking west over the valley watching the sunset. It was gorgeous. He had a beer at his elbow, he was naked, and it was warm, but not hot.

Then Sandy came out of the house, naked also, and she laid down next to him on the double chaise lounge.

They made love as the sun set below the Shenandoah, and into the night.

Carl woke up and wasn't sure he actually had. It was pitch black. Crap, "What did I do now?" He thought he must be back in the block, but he realized he could move and was still in the bed. He got up and felt his way to the door of his room. "Derek?" he whispered. "Derek?"

"Yeah Carl, what the hell….what's going on?"

"I don't know, I just woke up and everything was dark. I don't even know why I'm whispering, it just seems like the thing to do."

"I agree" said Derek.

It was at that moment that Ther-Leh came in. They couldn't see him at first because he was also dark. Once he got in the room he let himself glow a little.

"Don't be alarmed fellows! This is something we do at times if someone gets too close to Plor-Jarj, before they've been accepted. We black out the entire planet, and with our black atmosphere, we virtually disappear.

139

An unknown ship is passing us and we will be back to normal before long. I wanted you to know what was happening. I have to leave though, because I lead one of the observation teams. I'll be back in a while with more news if there are any problems, otherwise, we should revert to normal in a bit. Goodbye for now."

He turned dark and left, leaving them in the dark. Carl and Derek both felt their way to the table to wait out the blackout. They didn't talk, and forgot about mind communication. They both thought it best to be quiet.

It wasn't very long before the glow returned to Plor-Jarj. It came back gradually, over a couple of minutes or so, or, so they guessed. Again, Carl broke the silence, "Well, that was interesting. I had never given thought to a whole planet turning invisible, as a defense. Guess it's appropriate though for the peacekeepers of the Universe."

"Yeah, I suppose." said Derek.

"An unknown ship," said Carl, "I wonder where it could be from, and the Gilfeng not know about it. It seems like they cover a pretty big area."

"But Ther-Leh said they've only explored about twenty-eight percent of the universe, so far. And that's more than three million inhabited worlds. That leaves a bunch of unknowns!"

"Yeah, I guess so. You know, I wondered about that when he told us that. Do they know how big the universe is? I thought the universe was infinite." Carl said, half questioning.

"It was thought so for a long time. But then scientists found, by calculations based on observation, that there is an end to it. It gets really weird though because what you see today, say, through the Hubbell, is *really* old. So when they look, and see what seems to be the end of the universe, it's actually where the end was four-hundred billion years ago. Right now, it could be twice, or half the size we think it is. There's no way to tell, for sure."

"I guess that's why I'm not a scientist, I can't wrap my head around all of the theoretical stuff, and looking at stuff from the past. Give me the good old present, something I can have an effect on!"

"I'm starting to agree with you on that point buddy." said Derek.

Chapter 17

Time went by. Carl and Derek were learning amazing things about the universe we live in. Worlds, civilizations, languages, and sheer distances between the worlds that are inhabited.

And, they were learning how to live in peace. It's not as easy as it sounds, to live in peace. There were a lot of trials for peace. But they learned how to face all of them.

One day Ther-Leh came see them.

"Hello Derek, Carl." he thought.

"Hi Ther-Leh." They both thought back.

"This week is going to be very important for you both. This week we are going to begin your testing. If you have learned your lessons properly, and I feel that you have, you'll be home in a few days."

Carl and Derek were stunned. It was so out of the blue, neither of them knew exactly what to say.

Carl asked Ther-Leh, "How long have we been here, in Earth time?"

"Seven years, three months, four days, sixteen hours, and twenty-one minutes. To be exact."

"Do you feel like you're ready?" asked Ther-Leh.

"Oh yeah! Definitely!" said Derek.

"Alright, rest up, my friends. Tomorrow we start."

Ther-Leh turned and left. Derek and Carl didn't know what to do next.

"We're going home, man. We're freakin' going home! Yee-haaaawww!!" Carl let out a couple more whoops. "Although, I'm gonna about miss some of the stuff here, but I'll get over it! I can't wait to get back to my mountain and terra-firma."

"I wonder how they're going to test us?" Derek asked out loud.

Carl stopped dancing around and looked at his friend like *he* was from another world.

"We're going to be home in a few days, and you're worried about how they're going to test us? Who cares! We've learned all they wanted us to, so we'll be okay. Right?"

"Yeah, you're right. I don't know why I was worried about it. We'll pass with flying colors, I'm sure."

One of the many things they had learned over the years was how to have private thoughts and block them from anyone else. Right this minute, this was a good thing because Derek was definitely worried. But he didn't show it to Carl.

They ate some dinner, drank iced tea, and talked for a while, before retiring. They woke up the next morning and wondered what the day had in store for them.

Ther-Leh came in a bit later and said it was time to begin.

They left the apartment and headed toward the center of the city. It was the same route Derek had taken to find Carl in the black block. He feared that was where they were heading until they made a left turn and continued on, deeper into the city.

Finally they came to a place where a huge plaque hung on the wall. They stopped.

Ther-Leh said "This will be your home for the next few days. It is the test center. You'll notice the names of a number of worlds that are represented here. You will all be testing at the same time, and interaction and collaboration are actually part of your test.

144

Everyone has been taught the same lessons and you will all be given many chances to demonstrate what you have learned in your time on Plor-Jarj.

Missions will be given by myself, my assistant tutors that you all know, and some Gilfeng that you haven't met. To pass the test, you must demonstrate that your instincts are to act as you've been taught, not as you would have when you first arrived. Good luck."

He turned and entered the test center, and Derek and Carl followed.

Once inside, Ther-Leh left them to take his position on a podium at one end of the room, which was about two-hundred feet square. There were seventeen other sets of beings. There was a large, half-moon shaped shelf suspended in the center of the room, which Ther-Leh called everyone to gather around.

He welcomed all of the students to the test facility and started laying down the itinerary for the next few days. He also pointed out that everything that happened in this room, would be monitored by a number of Gilfeng. This included, very importantly, all thoughts and feelings. He told them not to try to hide thoughts from the monitors, they will see right through them and you will lose credits for every instance.

145

They would gain credits by accomplishing the tasks given them successfully.

"You're testing begins now. Today you must meet all of the other students in the room. You should be able to recognize all of the lifeforms in here, and be able to communicate in both their language and your own.

You are to talk to them to find out some of their personal likes and dislikes, things about their homes not in the lessons, and a key point that you must remember for all of your fellow students. At the end of this exercise, you'll be interviewed as a team, to see how much you remember. You may start now."

Carl and Derek turned to two slender, silver beings called Lefloriinge. They greeted them in English and Leflor, giving their names. They were from the planet Olglifonita, which Carl and Derek knew was a gas giant with a methane and hydrogen atmosphere, and a solid core of berrylium. The Lefloriinge were made up of berrylium and carborundum, with a bit of mercury thrown in. They like space travel and seeing new places, and they don't like their planet getting hit by asteroids, which happens a lot, causing many deaths. One thing they didn't know, Lefloriinge have found another inhabited world, have mated with beings from there, and produced offspring.

146

The other world is a small planet called Trasfagsm. It is in a solar system who's star is growing and devouring the planets in the system. The Lefloriinge offered to take all of the population of Trasfagsm to Olglifonita to live, and saved them all.

These talks went on all day until every set of beings had had time with all of the other sets of beings. Then the interviews started. They were questioned about beings they had met, what they had learned from them, the key points they had remembered, some things from this race, and some things from that race.

All of the beings did well and earned an appropriate number of credits except for the Bagrontijutes of Palyclidor. They had a difficult time communicating with some of the other students and couldn't recall enough information to receive the required minimum point level. They had to leave the testing sessions.

Nobody had thought that you could be eliminated at any time during the testing to go back for more training.

At the end of the day, they all went to miniature replicas of their apartments, in the test center, to eat and relax in their own ways.

Carl and Derek? They ate and talked for a while about all the interesting creatures they had met, and the things they had found out.

It was so wild to them to meet all of these other beings from different worlds. They finally went to sleep, wondering what tomorrow would bring. Tomorrow started about nine hours after they had gone to sleep. All of the beings were awakened and allowed to eat, if they were into that sort of thing, and prepare themselves for the next test session.

They were called into the main hall again and Ther-Leh explained today's session.

"Today," he thought "will be an exercise to check your mental reflexes. You are going to run into beings today that you will know nothing about. They will be from newly discovered planets, in many phases of evolution. Your test will be to deal with these beings according to the lessons you've been taught. You probably notice the large ring in the middle of the room today. This is where your encounters will take place, one team at a time. You all know Vla-Hurd, he'll be calling you into the arena for your tests. Good luck."

Vla-Hurd moved to the podium as Ther-Leh moved away.

"Hello everyone." he said. "Lets get started. Will the team from Drangaflatch 3, the Kilimnichuks, move to the arena, please."

Carl and Derek liked these two. They were one of the closest to being humanoid than any of the other races here. Even their language was very similar to Earth languages. They were only about 4 feet tall, one male, one female, and they were neighbors, almost. Drangaflatch was a small planet right at the edge of the Milky Way.

They entered the ring as a large box was being wheeled to the edge of the ring and a door on the end was slid open to the right. Everyone in the room drew a sharp breath when the creature came out. It was a Phnoomoret from a planet near the Tarillion system, called Phalgrod. No one in the room knew anything about it. The Phnoomoret was about five feet to the top of it's back. It had a large bulbous body, kind of like a spider, but more angular. Four hairy legs and a head that looked like nothing but teeth. Hundreds of them, all razor sharp.
The Kilimnichuks froze with fear. Big mistake. The creature jumped across the ring in one leap, and bit off the head of the female. The male fell to the floor in fear, and was immediately eaten.

149

Vla-Hurd entered the ring and using mind sway, backed the creature back into his cage.

The cage was wheeled away in silence.

Vla-Hurd went back to the podium without a thought.

"I hope you've all learned something here. You must remember your lessons, the things we have taught you. You cannot rely on your old ways of thinking. The next team is the Bulgrahar from Vralggend. Move into the arena please."

Needless to say, the Bulgrahar were in none too big a hurry to get into the ring. But, in they went. They were beings composed of a gas called shinsist. It is very lightweight and dark blue. They don't really have any features to speak of, and are blind. But they have thousands of motion and light sensors on themselves.

A box was wheeled to the arena and the door slid open. A whirling green flame came flying out of the box and stood in the middle of the ring. Carl and Derek were amazed at the diversity, even with all of their studies. This new being was a Frijolt from a planet called Frijolt. As this whirling flame stood in the middle of the ring, the Bulgrahar got on each side of it and mentally asked the Frijolt what it would like.

The whirling started to slow until it finally stopped whirling and just stood as a column of flame.

The Frijolt said that he really just wanted peace. His planet had been at war with a planet called Ormunub for two-hundred thousand years. He really just wanted to know what it would be like to live without fear. The Bulgrahar told him that perhaps the Gilfeng could help. And in fact, they could. The Frijolt was led away by a couple of Gilfeng.

Vla-Hurd congratulated the Bulgrahar for passing their test. "Next up are the Humans from Earth. Please enter the ring."

Carl and Derek tried to remember everything they had learned over the last seven years in an instant. Then they saw the box being wheeled to the ring. It was small, about two feet square. Derek sent out thoughts towards the box and mentally connected with the occupant inside. Even though he had no idea who, or what was in it, he found that they could understand each other. When the box opened, he got to meet the little Trchachl from Mywksla. Carl, Derek, and the Trchachl sat at the table that was in the ring and engaged in mental conversation for about ten minutes.

At the end of the talk, Derek turned to Vla-Hurd and said that Grpetch would like to know when they would be training someone from his planet about universal peace. Vla-Hurd said that they still needed to gather more information about his planet and peoples, and in fact, weren't even monitoring them yet. Grpetch thanked him and was led off by two Gilfeng. Vla-Hurd congratulated Derek and Carl.

This series of tests went on for another two hours or so. One more being, one of the Cysanhdy from Fejiging, was killed by a creature with a stinger he kept hidden. The other Cysanhdy thought the being back to his box. Vla-Hurd gave him congratulations and condolences.

Vla-Hurd told all of the students at the end of the day, to mentally prepare themselves for the next test session. It was most likely going to shock them. Of course, after the events of the last two days, every one was on edge, big time!

The next session when everyone came into the arena, Vla-Hurd directed everyone to go to the table bearing their logo.

"Today's lesson is going to help us predict how well you'll do at convincing the population on your home planets, what you've been up to. So, get ready to meet up with some friendly faces."

Some beings entered the arena from the far end and started walking towards the group at the tables. Carl immediately picked Sandy out of the crowd, naked and beautiful. No way, thought Carl, I must be hallucinating. Right then Derek recognized her and nudged Carl. "Look, it's Sandy" he said. "Yeah, I see her."

By now, all of the students were buzzing and their comrades had reached the tables. Sandy walked up and gave Carl and Derek a big hug and then asked, "What the hell is going on?"

"Are you real, or are you a cyborg?" Carl asked.

"What kind of question is that? And where are we? I was in my lab at M.I.T. one minute, next thing I know, I'm here, naked, wherever here is. Are these the Alnitaks we've been watching or what?"

"Yes, but their actually known as Gilfeng. And I had a run in with a cyborg, and just wanted to make sure it was you." said Carl. "Sandy, you wouldn't believe what we've been through. It's amazing. We've actually been here for over seven Earth years. This planet is called Plor-Jarj. The Gilfeng are the peace police of the universe, which has way more life in it than we ever thought. And-"

"Hold it cowboy" said Sandy "this is too much all at once.

153

Like, what do you mean you've been gone for seven years, I just saw you both two days ago. And what are all of these other creatures? And what do you mean this planet?"

"Okay, let me try to explain. You are on Plor-Jarj. It's the third planet from Alnitak. This is where the Gilfeng train beings from all over the universe, how to live in peace with the other beings in the universe. Apparently they brought you here as part of their evaluation of what we've learned. We have been here for seven years, but the Gilfeng are time travelers. Remember how we watched them on our tracking equipment and we couldn't see them until they got to a certain point in the galaxy? We always thought they were just out of range. Actually, they came in so fast, we just couldn't detect them. And on Earth, we've actually been gone for over a million years. Anyway, these other creatures are also undergoing their evaluations. They've cataloged some three million inhabited worlds, and have only explored about twenty-eight percent of the known universe. Isn't it incredible?!?"

Sandy gave Carl a long look. Then she looked at Derek. Quietly she asked him "Has he lost his mind?"

Derek simply answered her with "No."

"Sandy, it's all true. You really are on another world. You got here on a ship that has unlimited speed. And you are part of what will become the 'Counsel of Universal Peace', when we get back on Earth. Our job, there will be five-thousand of us once we call them all together, will be to convince the powers that be, that peace, is the order of the universe. Here, wait, let me try something."

Then Carl started to use mindsway on Sandy. In a few seconds, he showed her all sorts of amazing things they had learned in their time on Plor-Jarj. He explained everything he could.......and she got it.

All Sandy could say was "Wow."

"It's amazing" she said.

Right at that moment Ther-Leh walked up to their table.

Without speaking, he introduced himself to Sandy, and informed the three of them that their testing was done. They had passed and would be going home in a few hours. Carl and Derek jumped up to hug each other and Sandy, damn does she feel great, thought Carl. To which Derek laughed, as Carl hadn't protected the thought. Then they both laughed and thanked Ther-Leh a number of times.

155

Ther-Leh told them they could return to their apartment and get ready for the trip home.The three of them walked back to the apartment and showed Sandy where they had been living for the last seven years.

Carl and Derek could hardly believe it was over. They were heading home, and with Sandy. That was an extra bonus, thought Carl.

But going home. Wow!

Chapter 18

They looked at Melij-Beneb for the last time before levitating to the ship. And then they were on board. They all stepped out of their suits and got back into their clothes. There were three comfy looking chairs in the middle of the room this time. Ther-leh told them they could sit for the ride home.

"Well, my friends, it has been a pleasure tutoring you. You've learned your lessons well, and I feel you will convince your world of how to live within the universe in a relatively short amount of time. A ship will never be far away, and will always be around to help you. All you will need to do is direct any questions towards the card, and we will act appropriately. I will see you again, but not for some time, I have a new class coming in and I have to get them settled in.

We are at Earth. Good luck and 'Welcome to your universe!'"

With that sendoff, all three of them were sitting in the lab.

They all sat quietly for a few minutes. Carl finally broke the silence.

157

"That wasn't all some kind of a dream was it?" he asked.

Derek pulled his card from his pocket and looked at it.

"No, I don't think so." he said.

"So then, what was all of that?" asked Sandy.

"I mean, one minute, I'm sitting in my lab at M.I.T., then I'm in a bright white room somewhere. Next, some *thing* tells me to undress and put on this suit that looks like a skin. Then I'm in the big room where you guys were. And I got most of what you told me, both in words and thought, but what really was it all?"

Carl asked her, "Were you alone in your lab when they took you?"

"Yes, why?"

"It just might be a little hard to explain if you disappeared and never came back. Well, wait a minute, no, I guess you would come back to the point where you left, like us. Actually, it's kind of wild that you came back to here, with us, instead of going back to M.I.T. I'm not sure why they did that."

Derek broke in at that moment.

"Well, I don't know why they did what they did, I just know they did. And I think it's about time for us to get to work."

"C'mon Derek, not even an hour's break. We haven't been here for seven years, or one point six-two million if you count the space time differential. I mean, can't we even go over to Nellie's for a cheesesteak? Ther-leh was pretty good, but he never could quite get the cheesesteak down. It's the rolls, you know."

For some reason, his last line was the one that did it. They all busted up, and Sandy didn't even know why she was laughing. But they laughed and laughed, till Carl started choking and Sandy pissed herself. They all eventually regained their composure and cleaned themselves up, changed clothes, and headed over to Nellie's.

Carl said he could smell the cheesesteaks three blocks away. When they got their sandwiches, Carl got lost and savored his like it was the best meal he had ever eaten. They were lost in eating, thinking, wondering what was to come for them. They finished up and went back to the lab.

Once in the lab they just kind of milled around for a bit. Surprisingly, it was Sandy who piped up.

"Okay, so I gather the first thing we need to do is somehow find the rest of the people with the chips, right? How do we do it?"

Derek pulled his card back out of his pocket. Carl pulled his out. He showed it to Sandy and let her hold it. She was amazed with it. "This is so cool" she said, "I'm actually holding something that was manufactured on another world! This is so cool!" she squealed. "Can I take this back to school so we could check it out? I mean, would they allow that?"

"We should probably wait a while, we have a lot to do with these things right now." explained Derek.

"Oh, well yeah." she said.

"So I guess we should start, eh buddy?" Carl asked Derek.

"I suppose."

They knew what was about to happen. They told Sandy, so she would understand what was going on.

Derek filled her in. "We will put the cards on the table, one on the other, in the same direction. When we turn the top card ninety degrees, it will signal the ship that is on the other side of the moon. It will come around to Earth and pull all the others up to the ship.

They will do an orientation, of sorts, by mindsway to get them all used to the idea of what our mission is. They will then tell them how to reach us, and put them back where they were . It will all happen in an instant, so no one else will ever know what happened to them until the time is right. Right here, right now, is the beginning of a change for the better for the planet Earth. Welcome to the universe Earth!."

Carl put his card down, and Derek put his on top............

and turned.

Chapter 19

At that instant, Dr. Hans Von Bruchner, Coorda Harflutz, and four-thousand nine-hundred and ninety-seven people from the planet Earth, found themselves in a large hall. They were all seated in large, comfortable chairs. There were absolutely no details to be seen in the room except for a podium and the bright white light that seemed to emanate from everywhere. In a moment, the light dimmed to a soft gold and four beings entered the room from nowhere, and one approached the podium.

"Welcome, people of Earth. More than half of you can probably guess where you are. The rest may not realize that you are at a place that you haven't been to since you were ten years old, and the chip in your arm was implanted. I am Ther-Leh. I think you'll all recognize me from your past." He stopped long enough for the recognition to take place. Less than half of the audience started to cry as they did remember.

Ther-Leh continued "Many of you know, or know of, Dr. Derek Yosam and Carl Haskins of Project Find Them.

They have been trained to lead you on your mission of teaching Earth to be a member of the Universe around you.

You will all comprise the Earth's "Counsel for Universal Peace". We wanted to bring you aboard our ship so that you would know that we are real, that all of the bits and pieces you all thought you remembered were real, and to eliminate the first of the hurdles Dr. Yosam and Mr. Haskins will have. When we return you to Earth, you must all contact The Project to see when and where you will have your first meeting. We will send you back now in a couple of minutes and you will remember all of this trip. Good luck to all of you."

In another minute, all of the Earthlings were back on Earth and starting to contact the Project for further instructions.

It was decided that a new Council center would need to be constructed to house an organization of this size. Derek purchased six-thousand acres in Nebraska, west of route eighty-three, around a little town named Mullen. It was going to take about eighteen months to build the center, the surrounding support system, an airport, a science center, and everything else required to have a new city grow in mid-America.

In the meantime, Derek, Carl, Sandy, and some more staff that lived fairly close, started to document all of the new "Council" members that were now contacting the Project. Of course a lot more explaining was needed for all of the ones who hadn't been previously found. This was all new to them.

Derek and Carl spent their time devising the training formats and order of information to be imparted to the new council members. Of the two-thousand plus people that were already part of the Project, there were one –hundred and forty-three teachers. They were all different subjects and grade levels, some college professors, and some scientists. The training program became sort of a group effort.

There were also more than four-hundred computer people. Designers, programmers, code writers, network specialists, and others, whose immediate job was to begin designing the myriad of programs and record-keeping software needed for a project of this size.

The rest of the crowd was comprised of doctors, lawyers, linguists, and people from all walks of life and vocations.

For the next year and a half, all of the "Counsel" members started working on their assigned tasks from their respective base locations, until the new Center was completed. Most had made the trip to New Jersey, somewhere along the line. Others got a visit or two from Derek, Carl, or both. By the time the center was done though, everyone knew their jobs and were ready to go full bore. Training of the Counsel members moved into high gear. Inhabited planets, star systems across the universe, the peoples of the universe, all of the things Carl and Derek learned on Plor-Jarj.

Ther-Leh even came by for visits three times over the next eight years to check the training progress. Unbeknownst to anyone else but Derek and Carl though. The whole thing was being run as a science research center, as a cover. Of course, Derek released some wonderful new inventions to the world. This would give him credibility when he attempted to bring the world leaders together.

The CUP (Counsel for Universal Peace) Science and Research Center was becoming world renowned for the things coming out of it.

Then the time came........to tell the world what they were really doing in the heartland.

Chapter 20

The day to tell the world's leaders was chosen.
January 1, 2023. Derek's reputation and fame
as one of the world's most prolific inventors, was
what they were hoping would entice the world
leaders to come to the center. Personal
invitations were sent out a year in advance. The
invitations, along with the center's work over the
last few years, made sure no one wanted to
miss this event.

 They were translated into every language
known and hand carried around the world to the
leaders of every country.

The invite to the President of the United States
looked like this:

Dear President Tingler,

The CUP Science and Research Center in Mullens, Nebraska,

*Requests your presence at the live announcement, of the most
historic scientific discovery in the history of the world.*

*Presented by world renowned scientist/inventor Dr. Derek
Yosam,*

On January 1, 2023 at noon, in the main pavilion of the science center.

Please contact CUPSRC.com for your travel and lodging needs. You need not worry about security, as the facility is the safest spot on Earth, although we welcome thorough investigation and inspection by your security detail. You may bring as large an entourage as you wish, and won't want for anything.

You will be joined by all of the leaders of the world as this is historic news.

The members of the Center look forward to your arrival with excitement and anticipation.

All of the invitations were exactly the same, as far as content. And the calls started flooding in.

By May 2022, almost 85% of the invitees had responded that they would be there. A half dozen or so, said they would be sending their most trusted representatives, due to health reasons.

They would be provided equipment to view the proceedings live, wherever in the world they were.

The remainder either hadn't decided yet, or were of questionable standing on the world stage. Among them were some of the terrorist breeding countries.

Of course there had been a number of discussions about these very same countries

But as Carl and Derek had pointed out to the people of the project, this is exactly what their mission is. If they can't get all of the world's leaders together, then the part about world, and later, universal peace, was in jeopardy. Among members of the project were some diplomats whose job it became to convince allies of the holdout leaders, that it would be in their best interests to urge these holdouts to attend the summit at the center. This tactic worked and by New Year's day, 2023, every leader of a country on Earth was in Nebraska.

And so came time for the announcement.

The doors opened at 10 am, and the heads of state of the world were ushered to their respective seats. There were overstuffed chairs and comfortable desks with built in speakers for translations. As soon as people began to sit, waiters started trekking the circuit of desks, seeing to the needs of the occupants. By 11:50, everyone was in the hall built just for this occasion. It perfectly held all 246 leaders.

At exactly noon, Derek walked on to the stage, where a chair, microphone, and bottle of water, awaited him.

He sat, took a sip of water, adjusted the mic stand, and began.

"Welcome, to the Center for Universal Peace, Science, and Research Center." A quiet rustle came from the audience who had no idea what the CUP acronym stood for until now. But he had gotten their attention, and he continued, "This is a day that will change our world as we know it, because this is the day that the leaders of planet Earth find out that they have neighbors.....alot of them." The rustle became a noticeable grumbling amongst utterings like, "Is he crazy?", "What is this?", " I came here for this?".

But it got deathly quiet when a sixty foot tall hologram of Ther-Leh appeared on the stage behind Derek.

"I am called Ther-Leh, on your world. I come from the planet Plor-Jarj, near your Orion constellation.

Over the next few days, Dr. Yosam is going to explain the procedures required for the Earth to become good neighbors in our Universe. Over the next few millennia, you will follow his staff's teachings to learn the Universal Code of Peace.

When you've met the goals of the teachings you will be tested, and if you pass, will be accepted into the Universe and will start to meet your neighbors. We will teach you what you need to know, as we have taught the inhabitants of some three million worlds so far.

So please, sit back and listen, and learn. It was a pleasure talking to you."

With that the image of Ther-Leh faded away. All that was left was a stunned audience......for a minute. Then the grumbling got more intense with shouts of fear and disbelief. "What kind of trick is this?, "You expect us to believe this crud?", "Is this a joke?", "Are we being attacked, are you helping them?".

"Please, people, I can assure you this is no trick or joke. What you just saw was my colleague, Mr. Carl Haskins, and my, tutor on the planet Plor-Jarj. Many, if not all, of you know who I am, and my accomplishments throughout my life. Many of the everyday things around you were invented by me. I'm not some crackpot who's going to tell you that I've been abducted by aliens, and then offer no proof of such a crazy statement. Because I do have proof, a lot of it.

That proof is what we'll be discussing, and you'll be witnessing over the next few days.

When we finish here, you will have seen and heard things that are very real, but you still aren't going to totally believe it all. It's going to take years, in fact, it's going to take generations before the idea that we live in a heavily populated universe, will become a realization.

What I need from all of you, is to open your minds while you're here. I want you to take on an attitude that anything is possible. Listen, hear, watch, relax, and most of all, allow yourselves to imagine Earth as nothing more than what it is, a small little planet, in an everyday little galaxy, in the Milky Way.

Now, the next thing I would like to do, is introduce you to my associates. Please welcome the Counsel of Universal Peace."

A large curtain behind Derek slowly opened up and exposed a huge amphitheater. 4,999 people, the members of the C.U.P., stood in unison. It was so strange because it was dead quiet, again.

Derek continued, "This is my team. Many of you will recognize many of the faces. Some of them are the best and brightest from around the world. Others are ordinary men and women that were chosen by the Gilfeng for one reason or another. Oh, and Gilfeng is the name of the beings from Plor-Jarj.

171

All of these people were taken to Plor-Jarj for an orientation, after we returned, and before we started the project in earnest.

As I said, this isn't a trick or joke, this is the beginning of a course of action we, as a world, must perform before we can continue any space exploration. Which raises the point, all space exploration must be shelved from this time forward."

The hall erupted again in shouts and yells in a cacophony of different languages. All of the leaders with space programs, which was about 1/3 of them, yelled the loudest. Space travel was just starting to become a viable and lucrative business. Some countries were rebuilding their economies with space tourism. Now to be told they must stop, was unacceptable.

President Tingler raised his hand to get Derek's attention. Derek quieted the crowd and said he would start to answer the first servo of questions, starting with the President of the United States.

Go ahead Mr. President, Derek urged.

"Thank you, well Dr. Yosam, I'm sure we all have a million questions, but let me start with a couple.

172

First, why must we halt our present scheduled space programs, and for how long must we delay?"

"We, as a society, have reached the point in our development, where the Gilfeng step in and intervene. They, are the keepers of Universal Peace. They have been doing this for millions of years, all around the universe. This stage of development I mentioned, is when we are getting close to naturally discovering life outside our planet, and as you may all figure out, if your honest with yourselves, if we did discover life on other planets, we would want to go to them and introduce ourselves. Then, if they had a resource we could use, we would try to get it, by force if need be.

This is what the Gilfeng are in the universe to stop. They teach civilizations how to live in peace. The universe is too big to have worlds fighting over things, like we do here on Earth. That is why they've stopped our space programs.

How long it will take is an unknown. They said that it can take thousands of years, if we survive that long. But, we could be ready in a few hundred years, it all depends on the human race, and how long it takes us to embrace total and complete peace here on Earth.

But, if you figure that we haven't gotten it in thirty thousand years, I wouldn't get my hopes up that we'll become all lovey-dovey in a few hundred. But when we do, the Gilfeng will test us, and if we pass, they will teach us the technology to travel the universe. A large part of that travel is based on time travel. Yes, time travel. It makes sense.

It wouldn't be much fun to cruise the universe if you were just going to have generations of people die of old age in space, and never get to see any of it."

"But," asked the President, "why should we listen to them and stop our space programs just because they say so?"

"Because they've already stopped our programs. When this forum started, they activated a force field around our planet at 62 miles up. It will remain there until **we** are ready. And I know, as do the Gilfeng, that not all of you are going to believe that, and will try to launch spacecraft. Please, if you do, make them unmanned."

This was too much for a lot of the dignitaries, and many of them got up to leave. The griping got noticeably louder when they found that they were locked in. Derek called them back to their seats.

"Ladies and gentlemen, this is not a choice, if we want to continue space exploration.

 This is how it is from now on. We will not be allowed to leave this planet until we can live in peace on this planet! It's that simple. Although, I know that's not *simple*, we've been fighting each other for all of time, as we know it. But when you leave time, as we know it, a universe full of wonder opens up to us."

His Highness Kimbawe Sukuru, from Zimbabwe asked "So we have to get all of the peoples of Earth, to get along, and put down our weapons, to be allowed to continue with our own space programs. How do we know, or maybe I should say, who can guarantee that our neighbors won't attack us, once we've disarmed ourselves?"

"Quite honestly, your Highness, no one can. As I said, we must undo habits that have been thousands of years in the making. And it may take thousands of years before we accomplish this mission. But none the less, it must be done if Earth wants to join the rest of the universe.

You weren't brought here to tell you things that may happen someday, or give you some options about how we should conduct ourselves in the future. I asked you all here to tell you what the human race has been waiting for, for years. That we are not alone.

175

We do have intergalactic neighbors. And they welcome us......when.....we are ready to accept Universal Law."

Chapter 21

And so the training of planet Earth began. It was a tough task. There were a few more rockets launched to see if this "forcefield" was really surrounding the planet. Sadly a couple countries launched manned missions, which of course, ended with losing some bright astronauts. But it seemed that it would take far less time than anyone thought it would. In less than a hundred years, most of the territorial wars had ended, and people were beginning to change their perceptions of life.

The people of Earth had seen time pass, but Carl & Derek were still the cornerstones of the peace movement, and hadn't aged a bit. They were both in their mid-hundreds now, which was stunning enough, but still looked like they always had.

This, of course, had a good bit to do with the attitudes of the upcoming generations, and their willingness to accept the tenets of the Counsel of Universal Peace. It would still take forty generations for all of the old hatreds to be totally eliminated on Earth. For every inhabitant to embrace total peace. But the Earthlings did find that they could live in peace and happiness, and that it was wonderful.

Earth was turning into a modern garden of Eden.

Peoples and countries that had wealth were using it to help underdeveloped countries. People were helping people. Life was good on Earth.

The Gilfeng had been observing the progress on Earth the whole time. So after a little under a thousand years, they decided it was time to test the Earthlings to see if they were ready to join the universal neighborhood.

Chapter 22

It was August 12, 2936. For all intents and purposes, it was a beautiful summer day. But all that was about to change. At 12 noon GMT, the entire planet went dark. Where it was daytime, it suddenly turned to night. Where it was night, it became even darker. There were no stars or moon, or anything in the sky, anywhere. All of the electricity in the world stopped. It was just dark. It was like the Earth had been dropped into a black trash bag. And that's sort of what had happened.

The Gilfeng had turned the force field around Earth opaque, and shut down all the power stations somehow. They wanted to see how the people would handle losing their light sources and they're technology. This was the first test.

None of the training for peace had prepared them for this.

Needless to say, it was total chaos for the first 24 hours. At the end of the first day, the Gilfeng let the people of U.P.C. know that this was the first test.

Nobody really knew what to do. The Gilfeng didn't say how long it would be off.

First, the seven world leaders flew to CUPSRC to discuss the next steps.

Earth had turned into a very different place in the last 900 years since the Gilfeng first came. There were no more countries, or borders. There were no wars anywhere on the planet. There was no poverty, starvation, or political strife. In the process of learning peace, the Earth had become a perfect socialistic society. Everyone that could, worked, after the proper training. Those that couldn't, the very young, the old, and the infirm or sick, were provided for. Currency was deemed unnecessary, and had become a thing of the past. Everything one could need or want, within reason, was provided. This part took a few hundred years to work out, but seemed to be working well. Once all of the wars had ended, people realized it was much easier, and cheaper, to live in peace.

This new problem however, was going to take a new direction in thought. Derek, although not a world leader, was the most respected scientist in the world, and had remained the top authority on anything of this kind.

His first idea was that they needed to figure out how the Gilfeng had shut off all the power on the planet.

He had already done that before the leaders had arrived at UPCSRC. They had counteracted all man-made magnetism on Earth. Generators and motors couldn't produce magnetism. Solar energy never really had gained popularity, of course with a black sky, it wouldn't help anyhow. Derek had assembled a team that was already working on chemical reactions that could provide power, basically, large battery arrays. He also assembled a team to try and figure out exactly how the Gilfeng had counteracted magnetism, and, how they turned the force field black.

He wondered why he never thought of checking out the force field. What was it? How did it work? But now that it was black, it became much more urgent. He wondered if Gilfeng mind sway kept him from investigating. Whatever it was, he was over it. He pulled together a special team to build a probe with every kind of sensor imaginable. He would launch into an orbit sixty-one miles up to find out what made the force field tick.............hopefully. It took three months to build the satellite and a delivery system to launch it.

It was a hard three months though. The people of the world were used to the way things were before the power went out and the dark came. Most people couldn't work.

Nothing was being produced. Some forty million people died. Another two-hundred million were sick, and getting sicker. Derek and Carl had called Ther-Leh to no avail. He wouldn't answer. They thought this was very odd. They also thought his first test was highly unfair.

The day of the launch came, and the rocket slipped into the atmosphere quietly and without fanfare. All of the rocket and satellite systems that would normally run on 400 cycle electric, were being run by lithium-ion batteries. The tracking and ground control systems were also battery powered. It was a very small rocket, as far as rockets go. But it didn't have to do a lot of work to get the probe into position. It was into orbit in less than three minutes, and immediately started scanning the force field.

The first thing the probe checked was make-up. To Derek's surprise, it didn't take long to figure out that it was made up of liquid crystals! It was a free-floating TV screen! Odder still, all of the molecules were negatively charged, and in line. Derek checked the findings three times. He couldn't believe this could be so simple. The force field was a LCD degaussing machine. It had to have some sort of power source. If he could figure it out, he could shut it off.

He had the team ready another rocket. All that went on this one was a small guidance system and a very large bank of batteries, with the anode and cathode exposed and right on top of the rocket. It was launched and Derek and the world held it's breath. The rocket made it to the force field and…………..there was the sun, and generators on Earth started to hum with power production.

At the UPC center, Ther-Leh appeared at the lab where Derek was monitoring the action. "I'm surprised it took you so long to work this out Derek." he thought at Derek. Derek was in no mood to hear Ther-Leh right now. "Do you realize what you've done? How many people have died during your *test*?", Derek yelled out loud. "What happened to peace, and no harm?"

"As I said, I thought you would have come up with the answer to this problem months ago. You had to find the answer yourselves. That is what the tests are. We present situations, you have to figure out the answers. You've passed the first one, even though it cost some lives."

"Cost some lives? You call forty-million dead and a quarter billion sick and dying 'some lives'?" Derek shouted out loud.

"On the scale of the universe? Yes, some lives."

"I don't care about the universe right now, I care about Earth." Derek thought.

"But Earth is part of the universe, Derek. Don't you see this. You act as if you know each one of them. There are thirty billion people on your planet. You can barely support all of the people you have as it is. You've cured most diseases, invented synthetic foods, & stopped all of the wars. Have you decided what you're going to do from here? Has anyone even given it a thought?"

Derek fell silent and didn't think for a long time. He was the top dog on planet Earth. Everyone, every where looked to him for all the answers...........because he always had them. But now, this question. He had given thought to the expanding population. But the last time was probably three or four hundred years ago.

Just at that moment another long ago thought hit his brain.

Space. The universe. Could the Gilfeng....

Ther-Leh laughed out loud. That kind of startled Derek for a minute. Then Ther-Leh told him.

"This was the end of your testing, and you passed easily. Your memory of a long ago mission returned, and you've figured out how to save your world.

As promised, our engineers will show you what you need, to travel the universe at unlimited speeds. You are ready to meet the neighbors."

Derek was speechless.

Chapter 23

The Gilfeng engineers came. About 2,200 of them. They also brought raw materials with them that couldn't be found on Earth, but were needed to properly build universal transports. Needless to say, Mullen, Nebraska became much busier. The Gilfeng had come in a relatively small ship, only 12 miles long by about a mile and a half. They chose to stay in their ship when off duty, but endured the Earth atmosphere very well while working. Derek had to buy more land. He needed it to build the ship construction facility which was to be 150 miles by 20 miles and 4 miles high. It was going to be the single biggest structure the world had ever seen. Dozens of small towns had to be relocated outside of the area the hanger would occupy. Most of the people that were relocated would work in the hanger.

Derek was still in awe at the size of the ships. But there were 30 billion people that had to be moved somewhere in the universe. Earth's resources were severely depleted. Nine-Hundred years of near socialistic society and prosperity, had caused almost everything to be used up. Gold , silver, lead, molybdenum, cobalt, were all gone.

If it hadn't been for the invention of synthetic food processing, starvation would have seriously cut the population. Thus the size the ships would be. Of course there would also be much smaller scouting ships, but the people transports had to be huge.

It took three years to build the facility. It was quite remarkable. It had to have a high tech climate control system to keep it from raining inside. There were highways, a lot were left from before the hanger, as were the existing train tracks. Trains moved bigger items, while trucks moved the rest. People commuted in cars and buses. It was, after all, bigger than Rhode Island.

Interestingly, the ship the Gilfeng were helping the people build, was vastly different from the Gilfeng ships. Ther-Leh explained that ships were built using materials found, or once found, on the planet where the beings came from. The great thing was that any starship, once fitted with an appropriate magnetic drive engine, could move through time and space, as easily as any other.

Derek was still amazed that the idea of the little magnetic drive engine he invented when he was 10 years old, had been around for millions of years. Ther-Leh said that almost all societies come up with it at some point in their development.

That's when they ramp up the space program, and when the Gilfeng step in.

And so it was that the first inter-galactic spacecraft from the planet Earth was beginning to take shape. It was a scout ship that would cruise the universe to look at different worlds, suggested by the Gilfeng, suitable for Earthlings. It was going to be very small, compared to the ships that would follow. It was just over a mile long, about 300 yards wide, and would have 22 levels. It would carry about 2500 of the project find them personnel from all walks of life. The farthest world they were to visit was 26,000 light years from Earth, and it should take 4 hours to get there if all worked well.

Even though Derek had been involved with the project for years now, he was still blown away by time travel. And the space travel which ensued.

Sixteen months later, the ship was done. The Gilfeng had trained the flight crew how to fly a starship. The ship worked flawlessly. All was readied for the people of Earth to go out and find a new home. Derek was excited, and worried. He was the mission commander, and the future of mankind was on his shoulders.

Chapter 24

It was April 15, 3436. The first scout ship from
the planet Earth lifted off, and disappeared into
the heavens. Earth's intergalactic space journey
had begun.

188